W9-BBY-316

GEMINI SUMMER

GEMINI **SUMMER**

IAIN LAWRENCE

Delacorte Press

Published by Delacorte Press
an imprint of Random House Children's Books
a division of Random House, Inc.
New York

Delacorte Press and colophon are registered
trademarks of Random House, Inc.

www.randomhouse.com/kids

Educators and librarians, for a variety of teaching tools,
visit us at www.randomhouse.com/teachers

Library of Congress Cataloging-in-Publication Data
Lawrence, Iain.
Gemini summer / Iain Lawrence.
p. cm.
Summary: In 1965, Danny's grief over the death of his older brother
Beau is eased when a stray puppy adopts him, but he soon realizes that
Beau is somehow in the dog, and sets out to make his brother's dream
of seeing a rocket launch at Cape Kennedy come true.
ISBN-13: 978-0-385-73089-1 (trade)—
ISBN-13: 978-0-385-90111-6 (glb)
ISBN-10: 0-385-73089-6 (trade)—ISBN-10: 0-385-90111-9 (glb)
[1. Brothers—Fiction. 2. Dogs—Fiction. 3. Death—Fiction.
4. Family life—Fiction. 5. Project Gemini (U.S.)—Fiction.
6. Grissom, Virgil I.—Fiction.] I. Title.
PZ7.L43545Gem 2006
[Fic]—dc22
2006001801

The text of this book is set in 12-point Goudy.

Printed in the United States of America

10 9 8 7 6 5 4 3 2 1

First Edition

For Skipper

one

The sheriff leaned back with his feet on the desk, watching the blond-haired boy. He was a little man with a sunburned face, with white eyebrows that looked strange on all the redness of his forehead. His cowboy boots had shiny snakeskin tops, and he sat tapping the toes together. There was a blob of blue bubble gum squashed onto one of the soles.

He watched the boy for a long time before he said, quite suddenly, "You ever heard of fingerprints, kid?"

The boy looked up.

"I could take you into the back there and print you," said the sheriff, "and I'd get what I want like *that*." He snapped his fingers. "I'd know your whole name and your address and everything."

The blond-haired boy had a dog beside him. He was petting the dog as he sat in front of the sheriff's desk, in a wooden chair with arms. The ceiling fan that turned slowly above him trailed shreds of cobwebs round and round.

"Now, is that the route you want to take?" said the sheriff.

"How could you know my name and address from fingerprints?" asked the boy. He looked at his fingers. "I don't think you can do that."

"Oh, you don't think I can do that," said the sheriff. "A real little Perry Mason, aren't you?"

The boy said nothing. He had said hardly a word in an hour and twenty minutes.

The sheriff sighed. He tapped the toes of his boots together. "Say, that's a nice dog you got," he said. "What do you call him, sonny?"

The blond-haired boy didn't answer.

"Aw, come on!" The sheriff swung his feet to the floor and slammed a hand on the desk. "Holy moley, what's the harm in telling me the name of your *dog*?"

The boy shrugged. "Maybe you should fingerprint him."

"Oh, that's funny. Yeah, that's just hysterical." The sheriff opened a drawer in his desk and took out a key. "You want to sit in the cage and tell jokes to yourself? Is that what you want?"

"I don't care," said the boy.

"Then that's what you'll do."

When the sheriff stood up the boy stood up, and the dog stood up beside him. They walked in a line through the office, past the table where the lady had sat typing till dinnertime. There was a police radio there, and a teletype machine, and a shiny kettle that reflected the whole room and the turning fan.

The dog's claws ticked on the floor. The boy wished the lady would come back, because the lady had seemed nice. She had smiled at him all the time—just smiled and typed and talked on the radio.

"You had your chance, sonny," said the sheriff. He took the boy and the dog down a flight of concrete steps, down to a corridor with a jail cell on each side. He put his key in a lock and opened a cell, sliding the bars across with a rattle of metal. There was a bed in there, and a toilet, and that was all.

"Empty out your pockets," said the sheriff.

The boy did as he was told, embarrassed by the things that came out. There was a rubber band and a bit of string, a bottle cap, an old penny, a plastic man without a head. The sheriff took it all in one hand. "In you go," he said.

The boy went into the cell. The dog followed behind him.

The sheriff drew the bars into place, then turned his key and pulled it out. "When you're ready to tell me where your home is, just holler," he said. He went up the stairs in his snakeskin boots.

The boy stretched out on the bed. His dog climbed up beside him, settling down with its head on his chest.

"Don't worry," said the boy. His hand touched the dog's neck, and his fingers buried themselves in the black fur. "We'll get to the Cape, and it'll be okay. It'll all work out when we get to the Cape."

The dog fell asleep. But the blond-haired boy lay awake, staring at the bars and the bricks. "We gotta keep going," he told the sleeping dog. " 'Cause we can't go back. That's the thing—we can't ever go home again."

He looked at the lightbulb on the ceiling. Then he squinted and tried to imagine that it was the sun, and that he was lying outside on the grass with his dog. He thought about his home.

two

The Rivers lived in an old gray house in a valley named Hog's Hollow. All around, in every direction, the city stretched for miles and miles. To the west was an airport, to the north an industrial park. To the south were glass towers and skyscrapers and freeways choked with cars. But down in the Hollow, it was quiet and calm.

There was a single street laid out like a worm on the valley floor, and only nine houses, all sturdy and aged like the great nests of American eagles. There were seventeen people, but only three children. There were six cats and one dog.

A narrow stream called Highland Creek flowed southward through the Hollow, creeping past the cottonwoods. Danny River liked to play there, building dams of sticks and mud. Beau, his brother, sometimes helped him smash them.

Their father's name was Charlie. But the boys and their friends talked of him as Old Man River. They imagined that he never knew, though Charlie had used the same name for his own father when he was the age of his sons.

For a living, Old Man River pumped out septic tanks. He owned a black truck with a huge tank on its back and a little cab at the front, and he wore green clothes and brown boots, and carried his keys on a jangling hoop at his waist. He could peer into a septic tank, like a wizard into a crystal ball, and see the lives of people. He could divine, in a glimpse, what they ate, and what they tried to flush away, and what colors they were painting their walls. "There are no secrets from the septic man," he'd say.

Then there was *Mrs.* River. It was as though she had slept through the early sixties. While other ladies were trying to dress like Jackie Kennedy, she looked like Eleanor Roosevelt. Florence was her name, but Flo she was called. Little Flo River, barely five feet high, talking sometimes like Scarlett O'Hara.

Altogether, the Rivers seemed a bit odd to the people of the Hollow, who saw that big truck parked in the yard, and the Old Man always tugging at his filthy cap, and Flo in her cotton dresses, and Danny wading barefoot through the creek. "The hillbillies of Hog's Hollow"; that's what the Rivers were called.

In the whole family, it was said, Beau was the only

normal one. He did well at school, and he read books and he wondered about things like pollution and the Cold War. Only Beau, it was whispered, would ever amount to anything. "But that Danny," women would add, "oh, that Danny—isn't he a sweetheart?"

three

Each of the Rivers had a dream.

For Danny it was to have a dog of his own. He'd wanted one since he was four years old, but his mother had always said no. "A city's not the place for a dog," she'd told him a thousand times. "Dogs come to grief in the city." But Danny kept hoping. He loved dogs so much that it was said in the Hollow that he was half dog himself.

For Beau, his dream was to be an astronaut. He knew the weight of a Titan within ounces and the distance to the moon within a hundred miles. He even planned his illnesses around the rocket launches at Cape Canaveral. After Gordon Cooper splashed down in *Faith 7* in May 1963, Beau went to school with a note from his mother: *Please excuse Beau's absence. He had a touch of space fever.*

Mrs. River displayed *her* dream in the kitchen window,

on the shelves above the sink. The upper shelf was the Old Man's, a place to show off the interesting things that he'd pulled from people's septic tanks. But on the lower shelf, Mrs. River kept her dolls. She had Scarlett O'Hara and Rhett Butler, all the figures from *Gone with the Wind*. How she loved that old movie! After all, it had changed her life. She wouldn't even *be* Mrs. River now if Charlie hadn't looked so much like Rhett Butler. No one else in the world knew this, but in a room in the basement, down by the washing machine, Flo River was writing a novel about the South. It didn't mention the race riots or murders or lynchings. "That's not *my* South," she'd say of things like that. *Her* South, like her novel, was full of ladies in wide dresses who sat fanning themselves in the shade of big porches, in the shadows of peach trees. Her dream was to finish the book and make oodles of money. She would move the whole family out of the Hollow and buy an old plantation in Georgia. "Down *home*," she'd say—though she'd never been south of Virginia.

And Old Man River? Well, he didn't have a dream until 1964. And if it hadn't come to him then, all the terrible events that followed might never have happened. It was the Old Man's obsession that started it all.

four

When Charlie River began digging in the summer of 1964, people thought he'd lost his mind. He went at it in such a fever, attacking the earth with his shovel. He tore up the whole front lawn, digging down through the sod, then down through the dirt. He worked in the daylight, and he worked in the dark.

On the first day of his digging, Mrs. River and the boys watched him from the kitchen window. They saw him flinging dirt as far as the driveway, his shovel like a catapult. They heard it grinding through the earth, scraping on the stones.

"He looks like Mike Mulligan," said Danny.

After the first ten minutes, the Old Man's shirt was black with sweat around his armpits, and black along his spine. A gray dust floated at his feet, and with each push on the shovel he grunted.

None of them would go and ask what he was doing. He looked angry, his face red, his forearms bulging. He was like that when he shoveled snow in winter, except his breath would be puffing white like dragon's smoke, jetting from his nostrils.

He worked until nightfall that Saturday, and started again Sunday morning. All through the week he kept at it. When he wasn't pumping septic tanks, the Old Man was digging up the garden.

five

Being the son of the septic man made life difficult for Danny River.

There were kids who called the Old Man's truck "the poop-mobile" and held their noses when Danny went walking by. They called him Polluto and Danny Riverbottom. And those were the kids who *liked* him. They never came down to the Hollow, they never called at the old gray house, but they liked Danny River a lot.

The ones who didn't—the mean kids—called him names that Danny could never speak aloud. He had once written the worst of them on an old matchbook that he found on the street, printing carefully in pencil, and then had thrown the matchbook from the middle of the big bridge, to watch it tumble into the Hollow. There were times when the mean kids teased him so much that Danny nearly cried.

Then there was Dopey Colvig—son of Creepy—who'd been living for a year and a half at the northern end of the Hollow. Creepy Colvig was a construction worker. He went to work every day, driving through the Hollow in his station wagon, in his hard hat, leaving his boy to look after himself. Not one person in Hog's Hollow found a single thing to like about Creepy.

But Dopey was worse. He had a huge empty head with no brains inside it. He talked in sounds—in grunts and howls—that no one but Creepy could understand. He was too stupid to go to school, and so he never left the Hollow.

Dopey liked things that were shiny and sparkly. He had stolen the hood ornaments from half of the cars in the Hollow. He had swiped bottles from porches and a pair of silver scissors from Mrs. Elliot's sewing basket. Everything he took disappeared into the Colvig house and was never seen again.

Older than Danny, younger than Beau, Dopey was huge for his age. He was meaner than mean. For no reason at all, he hated Danny River, and he guarded his end of the Hollow like a troll, lurking on the paths through the cotton-woods, waiting for Danny to pass. At any moment he might leap from the bushes or jump up from the wooden bridge. Once he chased Danny through the woods with a realtor's sign, swinging it like a broadaxe, smashing through the bushes on Danny's heels.

Danny had grown up in Hog's Hollow. He had lived there since he was three months old, so it was the only place he knew. But it had changed for him when the Colvigs arrived, and he kept hoping they would move on, as they had always been moving on. Ever since Dopey had arrived, it was like having an ogre living at the end of the Hollow, blocking the trails that led to the heights and the school. For the last year and a half, Danny hadn't once walked along there without being afraid that Dopey would catch him. He only felt safe with Beau at his side.

six

Through the last, long weeks of the summer of 1964, Danny and Beau were never apart. They built a fort in the woods, and each swore to the other that they would never tell anyone where it was. "Not even under torture," said Beau. They rode their bikes to the swimming pool and down to the park.

One day they went looking for bottles, to cash them in at Kantor's store.

They went up Highland Creek. Danny tied his shoes around his neck and waded through the stream. When they came across a shopping cart upended in a pool, they dragged it out to carry the bottles.

They found thirty-seven altogether, nearly one for every yard of creek. Beau said it was like digging for gold in the Klondike. Then Danny said when he got a dog he'd maybe call it Klondike.

Beau laughed. "Yeah, sure."

"It's a good name," said Danny. He was rinsing out a bottle in the stream.

"Yeah, but you might as well forget it, Danny. Mom's never going to let you have a dog." Beau stood up like a charioteer on the back wheels of the shopping cart. "You should be bugging the Old Man, not Mom."

"Aw, the Old Man doesn't want a dog." Danny shook the bottle empty and brought it up the bank.

"He had one once. In the navy," said Beau. "I seen a picture."

"*Where?*" said Danny, unbelieving.

"In the green box."

"Yeah, sure. You never looked in there," said Danny.

"I did so." Beau stepped off the wheels, took the bottle, and put it in among the others. "I looked *all* through the box."

" 'Fraid nay," said Danny.

" 'Fraid so, Bozo! It was a black dog with white legs."

Danny waded through the creek as his brother pushed the cart. They were coming near the little wooden bridge where Dopey Colvig often waited.

"That's why Dad's digging, you know," said Beau.

"Yeah, sure. Because of his black *dog* with white *legs*." Danny made a spitting sound as he kicked at the mud.

"No, because of the war," said Beau. "I don't know, exactly. But I think that's why, because of what he saw in the war."

"You don't *know* what he saw," said Danny. "Nobody knows."

"Yeah, but it made people weird. Like Mr. Kantor," said Beau. "You know Steve Britain? His dad wets his bed."

Danny giggled. "He told you that?"

"Yeah."

"Holy man," said Danny. "If the Old Man wet his bed, I wouldn't tell anyone. Not anyone."

"Steve's dad wakes up screaming sometimes," said Beau. He got Danny to help him push the cart up the hill. "This one time, Steve woke him up in his chair, and he took hold of Steve and threw him against the wall."

"No fooling?" said Danny.

"I seen the bruises."

"Holy man." Danny shook his head. "It makes the Old Man look sort of normal."

seven

They wheeled the cart from the Hollow to the streets. Danny thought it was like coming out of the wilderness, as though they were Lewis and Clark. He had to walk ahead, guiding the cart, because it kept turning by itself.

It was a block to Kantor's. The boys pushed the cart right inside, and Mr. Kantor got up from his stool behind the cash register.

"Oy, it's you?" he said. "And I thought my day wouldn't be exciting?" Everything that Mr. Kantor said sounded like a question. "Did you rinse those bottles?"

"Yes," said Danny.

"You couldn't have rinsed your feet?" said Mr. Kantor. "You think the store sweeps itself?"

Danny looked down. Flakes of mud were falling from his legs and his trousers, from the wheels of the cart and its metal frame. Mr. Kantor was like a kind man hiding in a mean one, and Danny felt bad about the mud. He tried to kick it underneath the counter.

Mr. Kantor examined each bottle, squinting over the top of his little spectacles. Six he pushed aside, shaking his head. "I should give you money for no deposit?" Then he took up a short pencil and licked its tip, and added numbers on a slip of paper.

The boys spent their money right then, filling little brown bags from the boxes of candy near the counter. Danny took jawbreakers that would change color in his mouth, and caramels, and a packet of Munsters cards. Beau picked wax pipes full of juice, and a yellow sherbet fountain that looked like a stick of dynamite.

Mr. Kantor stood above them with his neck bent like a buzzard's, but he kept smiling. "Have you got your dog yet, Danny?" he asked.

"No," said Danny, counting out caramels.

"What are your parents thinking? Every boy should have a dog," Mr. Kantor said. "Dogs are always your friend no matter what. Dogs are good. People, they can be animals, you know. Trust me, I've seen it."

He emptied the bags that the boys had filled, and counted the candies. Danny watched his long fingers rolling the jawbreakers, and couldn't help staring at the blue numbers tattooed on Mr. Kantor's arm. He'd always wanted to know why they were there but hadn't yet felt brave enough to ask.

The boys left with the cart, their six rejected bottles

rattling inside. At the top of the hill, where the path led into the woods, Beau told Danny, "Get in."

Danny didn't want to at first, but Beau insisted; he said it would be fun. So Danny clambered into the cart and wedged himself along its length. Then Beau pushed it forward an inch, drew it back another.

"Three, two, one," he counted, and Danny shouted, "Ignition!"

"Blastoff!" said Beau, and down the hill they went.

The cart veered madly, tilting round the corners. It crashed through a bush and leapt from a root, and the bottles bounced round Danny's knees. It very nearly went tumbling over the cliff—thirty feet down to the creek—but skidded aside at the last moment. Beau came stumbling behind it, his arms straight out; he could hardly keep up with the cart.

Danny hurled the bottles at trees and boulders. They spun into bushes, bounded up, and spun again, and before they stopped he was past them.

He shot over the bridge on two wheels. Then the path went uphill, and he was airborne at the top, flying for a moment with the last two bottles floating weightless beside him. Then he landed with a crash and kept going, out of the woods, onto the grass beside the road. He thought the cart would carry him clear across it, so he cried out for Beau to stop him. He was heading for the Colvig house.

He looked back but couldn't see Beau. The cart bounced and rattled over the boulevard, and Danny now was truly frightened. He imagined rattling across the street and up the

Colvigs' driveway, smashing into Creepy's garage. But suddenly, like a miracle, the cart flopped on its side and spilled him onto the grass.

Beau came up a moment later, panting and laughing, and collapsed at Danny's side. Danny could hardly believe he'd ridden the whole hill; no one had ever done it before. He told Beau what it had been like to shoot over the bridge. And Beau told him how he had looked from behind—like Colonel Steve Zodiac. "Like Colonel Zodiac!" Beau shouted.

Danny held up the last of the bottles. "Watch, Beau!" he shouted, winding up with his arm. He cried, *Achtung!* like one of the little blue Nazis in the *G.I. Combat* comics, and lobbed the bottle—now a hand grenade—high and far. It twinkled in the sunlight as it spun end over end, then exploded on the road into a million white shards that skittered across the pavement. "Kaboom!" cried Danny.

They righted the cart. The front had dented inward, and they tried to bend it out again. Then Danny looked up and said, "Uh-oh."

Beau swallowed. "Creepy Colvig."

The man came across the road in his shorts and sleeveless undershirt. His arms and legs were covered with black hair, and his muscles—and his stomach—bulged. He was carrying a shovel on his shoulder.

Danny had never been so close to Creepy Colvig before. He could smell the man's sweat and see how his hairs sprouted right through his undershirt in places.

"Who busted that bottle?" said Creepy Colvig.

"I guess I did," said Danny.

"Then guess who'll clean it up."

Creepy Colvig threw down the shovel. He made sure that Danny found every speck of the million shards. "Sweep them up!" he ordered. "Put them in the shovel."

Danny was crying before he was halfway finished. He had to get down on his knees and gather the glass with his bare hands. He could feel it digging into his skin, and as he crawled back and forth his jawbreakers and caramels dribbled from his pockets. His eyes were blurred with tears, but wherever he turned he saw Creepy's feet in front of him, in sandals with straps, in white socks that had fallen in rolls round his ankles. Beau was just standing there, not saying anything.

When at last he stood up, when Creepy went off with the shovel full of glass, Danny's knees were scraped and white. Like his hands, they were bleeding.

He didn't say a word to Beau all the way home. They didn't even bother with the cart; they just left it in the grass. Beau put his arm on Danny's shoulder.

They found the Old Man digging. It was after five o'clock and he was home. Almost knee deep in the ground, he looked up. "Danny boy, what have you been doing?" he asked.

"It was Creepy Colvig," said Danny. His eyes started blinking; he couldn't help it. Then suddenly he was blubbering, with his nose running and his face feeling hot as fire. "Creepy Colvig made me—"

"*Mister* Colvig," said the Old Man. He didn't care for Mr. Colvig any more than anyone else in the Hollow, but he hated that nickname.

"Yeah," said Danny. "He made me pick up broken glass, 'cause I smashed a bottle, Dad. He made me pick up all the pieces."

"He did, did he?" The Old Man let his shovel fall. He came and knelt in front of Danny, then grabbed Danny's hands and looked at the palms. "Were you there, Beau?"

"Yes," said Beau.

"What did you do?"

Beau's answer was so quiet that he had to say it twice, and then his voice was still tiny. "Nothing," he said, looking down at the dirt.

"Why not?" said the Old Man.

"I was scared of him, Dad." It looked as though Beau, too, might start to cry. "I wanted to, but . . ." He shrugged.

"That's all right, son." The Old Man stood up. He gave his cap a twist, then climbed from the hole. "You two go inside," he said. "Get your mother to look at those hands, Danny."

He turned his back, and off he went in his jangling walk, with a streak of black sweat down his spine. Danny wiped his eyes and his nose. "He'll fix him, won't he, Beau? He'll teach him a thing or two."

"Yeah," said Beau. He looked up at the sky.

"Creepy won't bother us anymore, will he?"

"He better not," said Beau. " 'Cause if he does, I won't

just stand there like a rat fink, Danny. I won't let him do that again. Not him, or Dopey neither. If they try to hurt you, I'll fight back."

"Yeah, I know," said Danny.

They went together into the house, and when Danny shouted for his mother she came thundering from the basement, plucked by the noise from her novel and the plantations of Georgia. She looked at Danny and, in her voice like Scarlett O'Hara, said, "Great balls of fire!"

Mrs. River told Danny to sit on the kitchen table. She sent Beau to fetch tweezers and the bottle of iodine, and began to pick bits of glass from Danny's skin.

eight

The boys never learned what Old Man River said to Creepy Colvig. They didn't even know he'd come back until they heard him digging again. Then Danny, a bit ashamed of what he'd done, was afraid to go out and ask.

Right then, he decided that he would have to spend the rest of his life in the south end of the Hollow and never go near where the Colvigs lived. As he sat on the table, watching his mother scrub the skin raw on his knees and his hands, he felt quite sad about that. He could never cross the little bridge again. He would have to use the big one instead, and walk nearly twice as far to get to school.

"Sit still," said his mother.

"Sorry," said Danny. He'd been squirming.

She opened the bottle of iodine. A glass dropper was built into the cap, and it tinkled round the bottle as she stirred.

"Is it going to hurt?" asked Danny.

"It might sting," she said, and it did. But Danny only grimaced; he made no sound as she smeared the iodine across his knees with the glass dropper. It felt tangy and sharp, like lemon juice rubbed into his cuts. Outside, the Old Man's shovel was scraping on stones. "You should help your father sometimes, Danny. And you too," said Mrs. River, raising her voice so that Beau would be certain to hear. He was in the living room, and the TV was on.

She made brownish, rusty streaks across Danny's knees and his palms. "I don't know what he's doing out there, but I don't like him doing it on his own. He's like a crazy man, all that digging."

"A dog could help him," Danny said. "If we had a dog, Dad could just show him where to dig, and then stand back and—"

"Fiddle-dee-dee, is that all you ever think about?" said Mrs. River, suddenly smiling. She gave Danny's head a little push, and he saw how her eyes were shining, and it made him happy inside. "One day we'll move to the country," she said. "We'll move down South, and the first thing we'll do is get you a dog. That was always the plan, to live in the country. To have dogs and horses."

"Then why don't we move there?" said Danny.

"Not enough work for your father." She looked out the window, then dabbed again with the iodine.

"But the Hollow's like the country," said Danny. "It's *nearly* the country."

"Oh!" she said with a little laugh. "Now don't you sound

like your father? He said the same thing years ago, when we first came down here. He found he could park his truck out front, and to him this *was* the country." She put the dipper back in the iodine bottle and tightened the lid. "Well, he's never known what it's like to have your neighbor a mile away. Sometimes I think this is as close to the country as your father ever really wants to get."

The Old Man came in then, so suddenly that Danny jumped at the sound of the door banging open. But the Old Man didn't look angry. He only got himself a glass of water, and he rubbed Danny's head on the way to the sink, and again on the way back. At the door, just before he slipped out, he said, "I found a burial ground out there, Flo."

Beau was gone in an instant, but Danny had to wait as his mother covered his knees with Band-Aids, all that were left in the box. She crossed them over each other, until his knees looked like pink baskets. Then Danny leapt down and ran out, his mother shouting after him not to get himself dirty. He scrambled to the top of the pile, and from there saw the bones right away.

Three skeletons lay in the ground, in a row that wasn't quite straight, and not level at all. The Old Man had uncovered them carefully, so that Danny could see how the yellow bones had once been joined.

The tiniest little body, with its tiny little bones, had been a hamster or a mouse. In the middle was a cat, set down in the ground all curled round itself, the way cats always curled when they slept. The big one had to be a dog, because it wore the loop of a red collar, now dark and moldy. The bits of a brass buckle were there, and a name tag shaped like a bone.

The Old Man glanced up and saw Danny. "You don't want to look at this," he said, shuffling sideways to stand between Danny and the bones. "Me and Beau, we'll deal with it, son."

"I *want* to see," said Danny, and he went down and crouched beside the dead dog. He didn't mind at all that it was now only bones. It was interesting to see the insides of a dog.

"How long have they been here?" asked Beau.

"I don't know," said the Old Man. "Thirty years if a day, I guess."

Danny pulled the name tag from the dirt. He could see that it had once been painted yellow, but now it was almost all rust. He rubbed it on his sleeve, then read the name—Billy Bear—and it made him deeply sad. He could imagine what Billy Bear had looked like; he saw him, in his mind, covered in reddish brown fur, much fatter than he seemed now that he was only bones. He could picture Billy Bear playing with sticks, or reaching up a paw, asking to be stroked. Then he started crying, and kept his head down so that no one would see, because he was very ashamed to be crying twice in one day.

Beau and the Old Man were talking about the tiniest body, trying to figure out what the mushy stuff around it was. "I bet it's cardboard," said Beau. "I bet they buried him in a little cardboard box. See, Dad, that dog was laying on a blanket."

Danny hadn't noticed that, but now he did. Only a shred of cloth was showing, but there were scraps here and there that had been torn away by the Old Man's shovel. It had been a yellow blanket, just the same color as the name tag. Yellow must have been Billy Bear's favorite color, Danny thought, and this his favorite blanket, where he'd slept each night for all his life, beside a bed or beside a chair, and now for thirty years in the ground.

It was clear then to the Old Man and to Beau that Danny was crying. His shoulders were shaking, and a tear fell from his face to land on the little name tag. Danny thought Beau might laugh, but he didn't. And the Old Man picked him up, lifting him right from the ground the way he hadn't lifted him in two or three years. The Old Man pressed him to his chest, and Danny smelled the dirt and the sweat, and he shuddered in his father's strong arms.

"It's okay. It's all right," said the Old Man, holding him tightly. "Danny, I knew you shouldn't have looked. Beau, go get the trash can, will you?"

"No!" said Danny. "He isn't garbage, Dad. He had a name—it was Billy Bear. What if he's sleeping here? What if he wants to be petted again?"

"Oh, Danny, that's not how it is," said the Old Man. He eased down to the earth, so that he was kneeling and Danny was standing beside him, still wrapped in his arms. "These are just bones, Danny. They're no more or less than what's left on your plate when you finish a pork chop. There's no feeling in bones, son. The part that was a dog, that's long gone."

"Where did it go?" asked Danny.

"I don't know," said the Old Man. "It's just *gone*. Like his heart and his brains and all that. See, Danny, they're gone. It's just dirt now, nothing but dirt. The bits that made him up, they make up something else now. A part of Billy Bear could be in a tree, or in the grass over there by Highland Creek. He could even be in you."

Old Man River rubbed Danny's chest with one hand, his back with the other. "I don't know much about it, Danny. But Billy Bear isn't down here in the ground anymore, I'll tell you that."

Beau was standing nearby. "Do you still want the garbage can, Dad?" he asked.

"Well, that's up to Danny, I guess," said the Old Man. "If he wants to rebury the bones somewhere else, that's fine with me."

"Why can't they just stay here?" asked Danny.

"Because they're in the way."

"In the way of *what*?"

The Old Man sighed. He gestured with his hand, to show Danny all the digging that he'd done. Then he pushed up his cap and sighed again. "Well, maybe it's time you know. Maybe I should have told you from the start."

nine

From his pocket, Old Man River took out a handkerchief. It was white and blue, with a crimson border, like an American flag squashed in his hand. He wiped Danny's nose, then folded the cloth and wiped his own forehead. "Boys, I'm not just digging here. I'm building a fallout shelter."

None of them knew until then that Mrs. River had come out from the house. She was standing just beyond the pit, at the driveway, where the Old Man's pile of dirt was smallest. She'd arrived when Old Man River was talking about Billy Bear, and had listened with a look on her face that was soft and tender. But that vanished now.

"Have you lost your mind?" she shouted. "A fallout shelter?"

"Now, Flo—" he said.

"Great balls of fire, Charlie. *Why?*"

All of Hog's Hollow must have heard her shout that word. Birds flew from the trees, and a distant lawn mower stopped mowing, and in the August heat there was such a stillness that Danny heard the crack of a ball on a baseball bat from the field far away. His mother stood there with her hands on her hips, and the Old Man looked as though she'd slapped him.

"Don't you read the papers, Flo?" he asked. "Don't you know what's going on in Vietnam? It's 1941 all over again, but this time it's worse. It will bring the end of everything."

The Old Man climbed up onto his mountain of dirt. He stood like Moses at the top of it, and the boys sat below him, and Mrs. River stared up from the driveway. "I see it coming," said the Old Man.

Danny was still thinking about Billy Bear, and only half listened to what the Old Man had to say. He'd never heard of Vietnam or the Gulf of Tonkin.

"This is how the last war started," said Old Man River. "It's how they all begin, I guess. A bit of shooting, then it spreads like fire, and there's no putting it out. But this time it won't be guns; it will be missiles. It'll be men pushing buttons, and it will all be over before you even know it's begun. For crying out loud, they might be pushing the button right now. Those missiles could be dropping out of the sky and—"

"Stop!" said Mrs. River. "You're scaring the boys."

"Well, they *should* be scared," said the Old Man. "We should *all* be scared. Then I wouldn't be digging here by myself night after night. I'd have some help."

"You need it," said Mrs. River. She was staring into the

hole, at the mud and the bones of the animals. "You think I could take the boys down there? Into the dirt? Do you think we could live in the dirt while a war goes on, then come up like—like *moles* when it's over?"

"It will be survivable," said Old Man River.

"*Survivable!*" she scoffed. "Oh, fiddle-dee-dee, you and your war talk. Come along, boys."

But the boys didn't come along. They stayed down there in the pit, with the Old Man towering high above them, and little Flo River looking sick with worry.

"You can't run away from it, Flo," said the Old Man. "There's nowhere to run to."

He came down from his mountain, then took up his shovel again. "And it *is* survivable. The government says it is. We'll have concrete walls three feet thick, a roof banked up with dirt. We'll have food and water, and we'll be safe here, the four of us. Darn it, Flo, that's all that matters. I want to keep us safe."

He kicked his shovel into the ground and pried away the dirt. He was going deeper. Danny started digging out the bones of Billy Bear, scraping with his hands around the edges of the rotted blanket. Beau looked at his mother, then at his dad. "I don't know what to do," he said.

"Help your brother," said the Old Man. Mrs. River turned and left, her shoes scuffing through the spilled earth.

The boys moved all three of the skeletons. They used Danny's old wagon for a bier, carrying each of the animals in a big cake of dirt. They dug one long trench behind the house and buried the bodies side by side. Danny got so caught up in the ceremony of it that he forgot his sadness about Billy Bear. He found blankets for covers, and made wooden crosses from sticks that he gathered in the woods. He sang "Jesus Loves Me" in time to the drumbeats of the Old Man's shovel.

When it was done, Danny still had the name tag that Billy Bear had worn. He got a piece of string from the kitchen drawer and made a loop to go around his neck. Beau said it was a creepy thing to do, to wear the tag of a dead dog. But Danny said that one day he would have a dog and call it Billy Bear, and then he would hang the tag on its collar. "I think Billy Bear would like that," he said.

ten

Old Man River took to his digging with a fever greater than before. He dug in the mornings now, before driving off in the pumper truck. He spent so long in the pit, it seemed to Danny that it was the only place he ever saw his father anymore.

All the games they'd played—there was no time for those. The Old Man would come in for his supper and go right back out again. He never sat and watched TV, never helped Beau with his model rockets or Danny with his construction sets and card houses. He didn't come in until the boys were asleep, so there were no more bedtime stories, and *Treasure Island*—half finished—sat dusty on the table between the beds.

The Old Man and his hole became a curiosity not only in the Hollow but all around the heights. It was a mystery to

Danny how everyone suddenly knew about his father's dream. Danny had told fewer than a dozen people and had made sure they all knew it was a secret. But crowds sometimes gathered, everyone staring down from the edges as though they were watching the fat polar bears in the concrete pit in the zoo. Once Danny saw Creepy Colvig driving by very slowly, his elbow poking out from the window of his wood-paneled station wagon. Even Dopey came and peered into the hole one morning, scratching his bottom with one hand, his round head with the other.

Danny thought the Old Man would be furious to be watched so much. But, instead, he often stopped his work to explain about the shelter, showing where the food would go and where he'd build the bunk beds. "I'll tell you what we should have done," he'd say. "We should have got together and made one big shelter for all of us." But Danny was glad that hadn't happened. He wouldn't have wanted to live in the ground with Creepy and Dopey.

The only person in Hog's Hollow who never went near the hole was Mrs. River. It might have been full of crocodiles, the way she avoided it. She parked her car on the road—her big Pontiac with its fenders and tail fins—and went in and out of the house through the side door. She tried not to look toward the window as she made dinner, as she washed the dishes, now in silence. Before the Old Man started digging, she'd sung little Southern songs as she'd worked in the kitchen. She'd sung about Camptown races and shortening bread, and Danny had loved to hear her sing. Now she never spoke a word as she worked, and never mentioned the pit until the thirtieth of August, the twenty-first day of the Old Man's digging. Suddenly she pushed the window open and shouted at him, "Will you never be finished with that?"

"Not until it's done," he said.

"Great balls of fire! How deep will you go?" she said.

"To bedrock," he answered. "I'm going down to bedrock, Flo."

That made Danny shriek with laughter. He was sitting on the porch with Beau, the two of them eating watermelon and trying to see who could spit the seeds farthest up the pile of dirt. Their pieces of watermelon lay on the ground like the ribs of a green animal. Danny laughed so hard that watermelon juice squirted from his nose, and that made Beau laugh, too.

"You're like a pair of hyenas," said the Old Man from his hole. "What's so damned funny?"

"Bedrock," said Danny, for a picture had come into his mind of the Old Man reaching Bedrock, and of all the funny people pouring out. He imagined Barney Rubble driving up in his stone-wheeled car, and Dino the dinosaur raising his head. "Yabba dabba doo," he said, just like Fred Flintstone.

That made all of them laugh, his mother in the kitchen and his father in the hole. Danny heard the laughter booming up from the ground and thought, for a moment, that they were just a happy family again. Then the window closed, and the shoveling started, and he felt the sense of something awful on its way.

eleven

Down in the cells at the sheriff's office, the boy heard a door open. He heard shoes tapping on the floor, then the lady's voice.

"Where's the kid?" she asked.

"I put him in the cage," said the sheriff.

"Well, take him out," she said. "That's no place for a boy."

It wasn't long before they both came down to the cell. The lady brought a donut and a bottle of Orange Crush for the boy, and a box of treats for the dog. The sheriff opened the door and let her in.

The boy ate his donut. He drank the cold pop. He said, "Thank you. That was good."

The lady looked at the narrow bed, at the toilet in the corner and the lightbulb on the ceiling. "Don't you want to go home?" she asked.

The boy shook his head.

"Why not? Does someone hurt you at home?" she said. "Is that it, Beau?"

"I told you twice that's not my name," said the boy.

"Well, it's a funny thing," said the small, red-faced sheriff in the doorway. "That's what the truck driver called you. Now, are you saying he just made that up, sonny?"

twelve

On the last weekend of August, Mrs. River cleaned her dolls. She stood on a chair and leaned over the sink, finding pleasure in the crinkly touch of the miniature clothes, in the softness of Scarlett's hair.

She saw the Old Man climbing from his hole, its edges now so high that he had to pause at the top for a rest, bent over with his hands on his thighs. Then he came down, and straight into the kitchen.

"Where are the boys?" he asked.

"Oh, Charlie, don't make them dig today," she said. "It's their last weekend before school."

"I know it, Flo." He twisted his cap, then took it off. "I was thinking I haven't seen all that much of them and . . ."

The Old Man seemed uncomfortable, as though he wasn't used to being inside a house. "I thought I'd take them with me to the dump. I should empty the truck; I've got to pump the taverns on Tuesday."

"Ugh," she said with a shudder. Even the Old Man didn't like pumping the taverns. Their septic tanks, too full of disinfectant, were nothing more than cesspools.

"So, where are they?" he asked.

thirteen

Danny and Beau were up in the attic. They'd climbed through the hatch in the hallway closet and dragged out the metal box from its corner. When Beau pulled on the latches, the lid sprang up half an inch, as though the box had ached to be opened.

The boys looked at each other; then Beau raised the lid all the way. They smelled old wool and mothballs.

In the box was a sailor's blue shirt, carefully folded with its big collar on top. They lifted it out, then a pair of bell-bottomed trousers of the same color, with buttons embossed with anchors. Underneath was a crushed-looking cap, a couple of old books, and a bunch of paper. At the very bottom was an album full of pictures.

It had a paper cover that was tattered and torn, and black pages as thick as cardboard, all bound with red string threaded through holes at the side. Beau didn't lift it out, but reached down and turned the pages over.

Danny leaned forward. Billy Bear's old name tag slipped from his shirt and swung against the box. "Where's this famous dog?" he asked.

"Just a minute." Beau was touching the pictures. They were small and funny-looking, fitted into cardboard corners. Some had bumpy edges. Others had turned into yellow fog.

Danny pointed at one. "Do you think that's Dad's ship?"

"I think that's the *Constitution*, Danny."

"Wow! Dad was on Old Ironsides?"

"Sure, he's a hundred years old. Don't be a dope!" Beau pushed Danny away. "He musta gone and seen it, that's all."

Danny leaned over the box again as Beau turned a page. "Look!" he cried, jabbing his finger at a picture of a sailor and a lady. "Is that Mom and Dad?"

"Beats me," said Beau.

"Bet it is. See what it says."

They knew the story of how their parents had met, on the day before the Old Man went overseas. It was one of their favorite stories, how their mom—drawn to the city to work for the war—had thought the Old Man looked just like Rhett Butler, and how *he* thought she was from the Deep South because she talked to him like Scarlett O'Hara. Danny loved how his mother had hoped and hoped they'd meet again, and how his father had suddenly shown up at her house ten years later, to pump her parents' septic tank. To Danny, his dad was like a white knight in a pumper truck. Now he reached out for the picture, to see what was written on the back, but Beau shoved his arm away. Danny cried, "Don't do that!"

"Then don't touch," said Beau. "You'll get 'em dirty, Danny, and he'll know we been here."

Danny knelt on his hands, watching his brother pry the picture from its corners. "That's not Mom? What's it say?" he asked.

" 'A girl in every port,' " said Beau, frowning.

"Where's the one of the dog?"

"On the next page. Just a minute."

Beau started putting the sailor and the lady back in place, but Danny couldn't wait to see the dog. He tried to lift the bottom corner of the page.

"Wait, I said!" snapped Beau.

"You're not the boss of me." Danny pulled harder. He put his head down in the box, peering under the lifted page. "Geez, there it is!" He could see the picture now, a sailor crouching on the ground, ruffling the hair of a laughing collie. "Man, that's peachy keen," he said, trying to snatch it out.

"Quit it!" Beau pushed down, and Danny slid his hand behind the picture, and the photograph of the sailor and his dog creased across the middle. A dark line suddenly split them apart, and Beau shouted, "Holy man! Look what you did."

"It wasn't me," said Danny. "You—"

He stopped and looked at Beau. He could hear the jingle of the Old Man's keys in the hallway below them.

"Oh, geez," said Beau. "He knows we're here."

"Maybe not," said Danny, in a whisper.

"Sure he does." Beau pressed the wrinkled picture flat, then closed the album.

From the hall the Old Man shouted. "Boys! Where are you?"

They put the books and papers in the box, then the crushed cap and the trousers and the jacket. They pressed them down and closed the lid, and the air hissed out round the edges.

"Danny! Beau!" called the Old Man.

"Coming, Dad," said Beau. He pulled Danny away.

As Danny fell back from the box he heard a small pop of a sound that made him think one of the buttons had fallen from the bell-bottomed trousers. He looked round the floor and down at his feet, but Beau was tugging at him, saying, "Come on. Come on." Then the Old Man started thumping in the closet, and he hollered through the hatch, "What on earth are you doing up there?"

"Just looking at stuff," said Beau. He clenched his teeth and whispered to Danny, "Come on."

They went down through the hatch where the Old Man was waiting. Beau went first, down to the shelf, then down to the chair they'd brought. Danny crowded behind him, for he didn't like to be alone in the attic, not even for a moment. It was too spooky up there, with the shadows and the silence. He slid over the edge on his stomach, and as he dangled above the chair the Old Man took hold of him and lifted him down. Then up got the Old Man, onto the chair, and he poked his head through the hatch. "What's up here, anyways?" he asked. "Been so long since I looked that I can't remember."

"Oh, nothing," said Beau, grimacing at Danny. "Just stuff."

"Yeah, just stuff," said Danny. He tried to smile, but he felt terrible inside. He kept seeing the jagged crease appear across the picture, and felt as though he'd . . . well, he wasn't even sure how he felt. As though he'd punched his dad in the stomach, sort of.

"Huh. It's a museum." The Old Man's voice echoed in the attic. "There's Danny's old Jolly Jumper, and your grandmother's hatboxes. That's the first little chair you ever sat in, over there, Beau. And look; there's my old navy footlocker. Just sitting there in the corner. Why, I don't recall what I even put in that thing."

The boys said nothing. Old Man River grunted. "Have to drag it out and see, I guess."

He knows, thought Danny.

"Yup, we'll do that," said the Old Man. "But not now." He closed the hatch above his head. "I'm going up to the dump, and I thought you boys might come along. Thought we might stop at the Dub."

It seemed to Danny that a miracle had saved them. It had been a month or more since the Old Man had asked them to do anything, and now it seemed the thought had come to him right out of the blue, at just the very perfect time.

fourteen

Danny loved to ride in the pumper truck, gloating down from its window as it roared and smoked along the streets. Poop-mobile or not, his best friends envied him that—or the boys did, at least. And what the girls might think . . . well, that didn't matter to Danny. He didn't give a hoot what girls might think.

When Beau went along, as he did that day, Danny always sat in the middle. He had to scrunch his legs sideways, to give the Old Man room to work the big gearshift with its shiny eight ball on top. But he never felt so cozy and safe as he did then, squashed between his father and Beau.

They drove up through the Hollow with the engine growling, and Danny held on to the eight ball so that the lever wouldn't rattle. He looked down on the roofs of cars, down on the heads of people on the sidewalk. Riding in the truck made him feel enormous, like the little Martians in their great walking robots.

At the top of the hill they turned right, over the big bridge with its metal grating that hummed from the traffic. All of Hog's Hollow suddenly lay below them, and Danny stretched up on the seat to watch his house flicker by in the row of others. His father's hand nudged his own from the eight ball.

The Old Man, in his coveralls and boots, changed up through the gears. The windows were open, and hot air blasted around them, so the Old Man had to pull his hat low. The truck surged and swayed from the weight that sloshed in its tank, and they went barreling through the city.

"So it's back to school next week," said the Old Man, and that sort of destroyed the mood. It seemed to Danny that a hole opened inside him.

"Now, I know I've been . . . preoccupied," said the Old Man. "With all the digging." His big hand rubbed the eight ball. "I haven't seen much of you, and I'm sorry. I promise that next summer will be better. Next summer we'll go on a trip."

"Where?" asked Danny.

"Don't know," said the Old Man. "Your mother and me, we thought we'd let you boys decide. So give it some thought and—"

"The Cape!" shouted Beau. "Cape Canaveral."

"Oh, that's a long ways, isn't it?" said the Old Man. "That's down in the Carolinas or somewhere."

"Florida," said Beau.

"*Florida!* Geez." The Old Man gave his cap a hard twist. "That must be a thousand miles."

"Yeah, I guess," said Beau with a sigh. He turned toward the window, and the wind pushed his blond hair sideways, then forward and back. The truck was roaring up the four-lane street, past Kantor's store, on to the north.

They went three or four blocks before anyone talked. Then the Old Man looked across at Beau. "The Cape, huh? Well, I'd like to take you there, son, but I can't see it coming that soon. Maybe two, three years from now. It's—"

"But Dad, they'll be launching six Titans next year; four Gemini flights. There's one in June and one in August," said Beau. "It'll be like Gemini summer down there. Can't we go, Dad?"

"To *Florida?*" The Old Man blew air through his mouth, and his lips made a puttering sound. "Well, I suppose if we *did*, then your mother would get to see Georgia. I suppose we *could* swing through Atlanta, and wherever that damned Tara place is." He pressed the brake pedal as the traffic slowed, and all the stuff in the tank seemed to shove at their backs. "Yes, it would make your mother happy, all right."

"She deserves it," said Beau.

The Old Man laughed, and that made Danny feel the truck shrink to a cozy tightness. He grinned at Beau, who was sitting up now, all windblown and red.

"When are the launches?" asked the Old Man. "Those Gemini flights."

"There's one in March," said Beau. "Gus Grissom's going to be the first guy to go twice into space. Then—"

"Grissom?" said the Old Man, starting up through the gears again. The cars were passing them. "After what he did the last time, I wouldn't let that guy fly a paper dart."

"It wasn't his fault, Dad," said Beau.

"Come on, he abandoned ship. Blew the hatch; lost the capsule." The Old Man put his arm out the window. His coveralls rippled in the draft. "Now, I'm not saying I blame him. I know from my navy days what it's like to bob around in the ocean. And him all alone in a tin can, well . . ." He shrugged. "No wonder he was scared. Who wouldn't have wanted to get out?"

"He *wasn't* scared," said Beau. "He didn't *want* to get out. He *had* to get out 'cause the hatch blew off."

"What do *you* think, Danny?" asked the Old Man. "Do you remember that?"

Of course he remembered. They'd all watched the launch on TV, and the films that had come in later. They'd seen the capsule—*Liberty Bell 7*—swinging down under its parachutes. They'd seen it rocking in the ocean, as though they'd actually been riding in the helicopter that had taken the pictures. They'd seen the hatch fly open with a puff of smoke, and Gus Grissom come tumbling out. Then the helicopters had hooked on to *Liberty Bell,* even as it was sinking, and it had seemed that the capsule would pull the chopper right into the sea. And there was Gus Grissom, floating around as his spacesuit filled with water, the poor man waving for all he was worth, but no one going to help him.

"I don't think he was scared," said Danny. "There's nothing in the world that would scare that guy, is there, Beau?"

" 'Cept maybe looking at you," said Beau.

That made Danny laugh, and the Old Man, too. The truck was filled with a happy feeling again as they drove out of the city, past the shopping malls, into a world of factories and vacant lots. They found the dump, and emptied the truck, then stopped at the A&W.

A waitress came out in her brown uniform and little paper hat. She had to stare so high up at the cab that she shouted, as though hollering to people on a mountaintop. The Old Man called down his order, then drummed his fingers on the steering wheel as they all sat back to wait. With a sigh, he slapped hard on the rim of the wheel. "Oh, what the heck," he said. "We'll go."

"To the Cape?" asked Danny.

"Sure. Next summer."

"I can hardly wait," said Beau.

fifteen

They took their food in a paper bag that Danny held in his lap, feeling the heat on his legs and stomach, smelling the burgers and french fries. He knew it was not to be opened; they had a routine.

They drove to the river, to their favorite spot, where there were a park and a waterfall. Danny carried the bag to the same place they'd gone the last time, and maybe fifty times before that, to a jumble of flat rocks made hot by the sun. They even had their own rocks—three in a circle, and a fourth like a table—overlooking the pool where people went swimming, where kids floated around on air mattresses.

On the grass at the riverside, there were families having picnics. A harried-looking man with a great potbelly was trying to fish at the foot of the rapids. The Old Man and the boys ate their burgers and fries, then crunched all the garbage into the paper bag. They lay for a while like lizards on the stones, watching big cumulus clouds tumble along.

They were just climbing into the truck when the dogs appeared. One came from the east, and one from the west, and they raced to the river together. They stood and barked across it, then each twirled once around and plunged into the stream. In the middle they collided and the water frothed, then both came bursting onto the grass. They stood nose to nose, their tails wagging, then each of them pressed its chin to the ground, like gentlemen bowing, and suddenly they sprang up and started running. Soon everyone in the park—even the potbellied man—was watching them run. The black dog led the brown dog on a crazy chase between the benches and the tables, through the trees and down the river. It snatched up sticks; it ducked and weaved.

The Old Man had his door open, one foot up on the running board, a hand reaching for the wheel. He stopped there, like a statue, staring through the frame of the rolled-down window. His head turned to and fro as he followed the dogs with his eyes, down the park and back again. "They're a couple of kids," he said.

Danny was already in the truck, in his place in the middle, watching through the windshield. "You mean puppies, Dad," he said.

"No, Danny, they're kids," said the Old Man, as though there were no other word for it. "They're little boys. No worries or cares; look at them. Little boys forever. I bet they meet here every afternoon and play some sort of game."

All over the park, people were standing up now. They were grinning at each other, laughing, as the dogs whirled in and out from the tables. The brown one chased the black one, then the black one chased the brown one, weaving between the garbage cans. Two little toddlers went trundling after them, and their mothers after *them*, and the Old Man laughed more loudly than Danny could ever remember him laughing. He had to wipe tears of laughter from his eyes.

Beau had watched quietly until then, standing up on the running board at his side of the truck. Now he sighed and said, "It would sure be neat to be a dog."

"I know just what you mean," said the Old Man.

The mothers caught the toddlers before the toddlers could catch the dogs. They swept them up, and people cheered. Then the black dog and the brown dog suddenly turned and dashed toward the river, bounding over the grass. They hurled themselves into the water—they *cannonballed* into the water—and the potbellied man was drenched with the spray. He threw up his arms and laughed with everyone else as the dogs vanished into the trees on the far side of the river.

Old Man River pulled himself up behind the wheel. "That was something, huh, Danny?" he said.

Danny nodded. "It was neato, Dad."

"If you were a dog, you'd be like that black one, playing and laughing all the day."

Beau moved onto the seat. "No, he'd be a wiener dog, the wiener." He closed his door. "How would I be, Dad?"

"Well, you'd talk a mile a minute," said the Old Man

with a chuckle. He gave the gas pedal a pump. "You'd go on big adventures and you'd sit and think on things." He turned the key, and the engine started. "You'd be a thoughtful kind of dog."

Beau seemed pleased by that. He put his head out the window and watched behind them as the Old Man backed up.

"Now, if I was a dog," said the Old Man, "I guess I'd want to be a collie." He shoved the lever into first gear and pulled out onto the street. "I always liked collies."

Danny looked at Beau, who suddenly seemed embarrassed.

"I used to have one. Did you know that?"

"No, I didn't know that," said Danny. "We never would have guessed, would we, Beau?"

Beau said nothing. The Old Man leaned forward and jangled his ring of keys from under his hip. "Yup. He was called Nelson. Looked like him, too. Missing one eye and one leg."

Danny frowned. He was sure that the dog he'd seen in the picture had all four of its legs. He wondered—how could it have moved with only three? Could it shake hands?

The Old Man grinned. "Oh, I'm just pulling your leg," he said. "There was nothing wrong with poor old Nelson. I called him that 'cause he was admirable."

"What happened to him, Dad?" asked Danny. "Did he drown at sea?"

The Old Man was working the gearshift, coaxing the truck up a hill. Without all its weight, it moved more quickly, and it didn't sway so much from side to side. "Now why would you ask that?" he said.

Danny had to swallow. "Just wondering, Dad. 'Cause you were in the navy."

"Huh. Well, yes, Danny, that's pretty much what happened. Except he wasn't at sea. He drowned in a puddle of water, no deeper than Highland Creek." The Old Man sighed. "He fell through the ice on Christmas Day, poor old Nelson."

"Gosh, that's sad," said Danny.

"Yup," said the Old Man with another sigh. "I've got a picture of him somewhere. Tell you what—I'll look it up when we get home. You might like to have it, Danny."

"Oh, that's okay," said Danny.

"Yeah, that's okay," said Beau. "It's not like he's going to call a dog Nelson, are you, Danny?"

"No," said Danny. "When I get a dog I'm going to call it Billy Bear." He reached up to the name tag, but his hand didn't find the string. He yanked the front of his T-shirt down and peered inside it. "Oh, no. Dad!"

The Old Man slammed his foot on the brake pedal. The tires squealed, and Danny nearly flew up against the windshield. Behind them, a car honked.

"What's the matter?" said Old Man River.

"I lost my name tag," Danny said.

"Oh, Danny boy, for crying out loud. You nearly caused an accident." With a shake of his head and a terrible sigh, the Old Man clenched his teeth. He pulled so hard on his cap that it covered his eyes for a moment.

Danny was searching frantically through the cab, down on the floor, and the Old Man kept ramming the gearshift into his leg. "Ow!" Danny cried.

"Get up!" said the Old Man. More cars were honking now. One crept past the side of the truck, and the driver scowled up at them. He had a cigar in his mouth, and a long mustache, and he looked like a smoking walrus. He tapped his finger on his temple, as though he thought the Old Man was crazy.

"We have to go back," Danny was saying. "I musta left it at the park."

The Old Man didn't even know that Danny had kept Billy Bear's little tag. Beau had to explain, because Danny was too upset to talk slowly. Then Old Man River said it was a stupid thing to want to keep, the name tag of a dead dog, and he wouldn't go back if his life depended on it.

Beau prodded Danny in the ribs. "See?" he said. "Dad, I told him it was a creepy thing to do."

sixteen

Mrs. River almost screamed when she heard the plan about Florida. Danny had never seen her so excited.

"Going through Georgia!" she said. "Seeing the South in the summer? Oh, great balls of fire!"

Danny liked it when she used her Southern voice. He watched her run to the calendar, and in a moment—on the page for the next year—she had ten days marked in for August. And that seemed to make it official.

"Oh, Charlie," she said, "I'm going home."

"Home?" The Old Man chuckled. "It's hardly home to you, Flo."

Nothing could take away her happiness. "My grandfather was born in Virginia. Y'all can't get more Southern than that."

seventeen

On the first day of school, Danny and Beau sat eating their breakfast, wearing clothes that were fresh and new. Their jeans were so tightly creased that it looked as though the Old Man had run over their legs with his truck.

"You look so smart, the two of you," said Mrs. River. She was eager to get down to the basement, to get back to her novel, and she hurried the boys along. "Now, Beau, are you sure you don't want to wear a tie?"

"Mom!" he said. "Only browners wear ties."

"Oh, fiddle-dee-dee. Smart young men wear ties." She wiped the milk from Danny's lips, then tried to flatten his hair with spit on her fingers. But he tilted away each time she came near.

Danny felt doomed. He could hardly believe that summer was over, that the very last moments of it were passing away as the kitchen clock went *tick . . . tock . . . tick*. It was shaped like a black cat, with the cat's tail for a pendulum, and its big eyes looked side to side with every tick and tock. Danny watched the minute hand jump forward. When Beau got up, so did he. They went to the door; they put on their new shoes. As Danny tied his laces he knew how Doc Holliday had felt as he'd dressed for the walk to the OK Corral.

Danny was laden down that morning. His pockets were filled with the best of the things he had found through the summer, the shiniest stones and the oldest pennies, the most interesting bottle caps—the things he would show off to his friends. He had to hurry along to keep up with Beau, and his pockets sort of sloshed, like the stuff in the tank on the Old Man's truck.

They were crossing the bridge when Dopey Colvig leapt out from the bushes, holding a stick as stout as a rolling pin. Feet apart, hands at his side, he stood right at the fork in the trail. He was half again as wide as Beau.

He made those sounds, those hoots and groans that only Creepy could understand. His great hollow head with its pudding of a face watched them like an owl's.

Danny pressed up against his brother. "Let's go back," he said. "Let's go over the big bridge instead."

"That's too far that way. You want to be late?" asked Beau.

Dopey came forward. He grunted and mumbled. The way he walked, he looked like a giant to Danny, though he wasn't really big enough for that. He looked like the world's smallest giant, ready to grind their bones into bread.

Beau didn't move. "Get lost, Dopey," he said.

Danny reached into his pocket of stones. He pulled out a round one that was red and fiery, like a blazing eyeball. He threw it at Dopey and hit him smack on his dopey forehead. The sound of it hitting was like a walnut bursting in a nutcracker.

Dopey's eyes blinked, but that was all. His eyes blinked, and he came forward again. He raised the stick and made a sound like a squealing pig.

"Oh, geez," said Danny. "I made him mad."

Dopey started running. It was more like a boulder crashing along, but he came down the trail in heavy, thudding steps, and he mumbled and shrieked again. Danny wanted to run, but Beau stayed where he was. "I think I can take him," said Beau.

Then a voice shouted out from beyond the trees, from the clearing down below. "What's going on up there?" it asked.

Danny said, "That's Creepy Colvig."

Dopey looked up at the sound of the voice, like a dog looking up to a whistle. And Beau hunched down and raised his shoulder, and caught the giant boy off guard. Dopey staggered backward. His left foot landed on the bridge, and his right went over the edge. Then he stumbled down the slope and crashed against a tree. The branches shivered. Leaves came drifting down.

Beau hit him again. "You leave my brother alone!" he cried.

Now Creepy was coming up the trail. Through the twigs

and leaves, Danny could see his yellow hard hat bobbing along like a big, fat chicken, and knew that Creepy had been on his way to work. A minute later, and they would have missed him.

"Here, you!" shouted Creepy Colvig. "Come down here and pick on someone who can fight back!"

Beau grabbed Danny and hauled him along, and up they went on the twisting path. Pebbles and pennies spilled from Danny's pockets. The sharp edges of his bottle caps prickled on his leg. He couldn't run fast enough, and Beau had to drag him up the steep part.

Dopey was howling behind them, while Creepy shouted, "I see you there. I know who you are!"

Danny heard a crackling in the trees, then a thud in the bushes. "Beau, he's throwing rocks!" he cried.

"Then come on, Danny."

They scrambled up the hill with their new shoes squeaking, their new jeans rubbing like sandpaper. The cries of Creepy Colvig seemed to chase them up the slope: "You're the River boys. You'll pay for this, you hear?"

eighteen

Danny took the long way home in the afternoon, and his mother was furious when she saw him come into the house.

"Look at your new clothes!" she said. "Your pocket's torn, your jeans are filthy. Tarnation, Danny, why do I bother with you? It would save both time and money if I dressed you in rags from the rag shop."

"It wasn't my fault," said Danny. "It was Dopey Colvig. Then Creepy threw a rock at us, and—"

"He *what?*"

So again Old Man River went round to "have a talk" with Creepy. Again, neither Danny nor Beau knew what was said, but suddenly the Rivers and the Colvigs were like the Hatfields and the McCoys, feuding away in Hog's Hollow. A bag of trash—nibbled corncobs and coffee grounds and chicken bones—appeared one night in the Old Man's pit.

The next night it was all spread across the Colvigs' lawn. Then Old Man River found the windshield of his pumper truck smeared with the yolks of many broken eggs.

There were people who found it all very funny. "The hillbillies are feuding now," they'd say, and laugh behind their hands.

The Old Man didn't worry. "I want you boys to keep going to school the way you always have," he said. "If there's any trouble, you just tell me. Not that I think there will be. Colvig's a bag of wind, and he'll be moving on again pretty soon, I think. He's worn out his welcome here, like he did at the last place, and the place before."

Danny knew all that. There was a sort of children's telegraph that had spread the story of the Colvigs and how they kept moving every time Dopey got in trouble. For Danny, the next move couldn't come fast enough. He stuck more closely than ever to Beau in the mornings, and took the long way home nearly every day. Beau stayed for football on Mondays and Thursdays and for Rocket Club on Tuesdays. On Wednesdays he had NASA Club, and that was his favorite. There were only three kids in the club, but Beau was the president because he had started it. "What do you do at NASA Club?" Danny had asked him once.

"We sort of sit around and talk about the space race," Beau had told him.

"For two *hours?*"

"Well, sometimes we just sit around and look at Miss Jenkins." She was the sponsor. She wore miniskirts and leather boots.

"Why?" asked Danny. "I don't understand why you'd want to do that."

"Well, that's why you're not in the club," said Beau.

Fridays were the only days that Beau didn't have to stay late. So there were just three days in September when Danny walked home with his brother, through the woods and down the trails, past the place where the Catholics held their Camp Wigwam in the summer. Danny came to love Fridays, but in October that ended.

"Don't wait for me after school, okay?" said Beau on the first Friday of the month.

"But it's Friday," Danny said.

"Yeah, I know, but . . ." Beau was just ahead of Danny, walking up the hill in the morning, with the birds whistling in the trees. "Danny, I just want to hang around a bit."

"I can wait," said Danny. "I don't care how long."

"I don't *want* you to wait," said Beau. "And I don't mean just today. I mean every Friday."

Danny was puffing up the hill, trying to keep right behind Beau. "What if we ask the Old Man to meet us on Fridays? Maybe he can come by the school, and we can go to the Dub?"

"No, Danny." Beau stopped on the trail and turned around. He was carrying his books in both arms, like a girl. He always switched them over to one hand when they came up to the street. "Don't even ask him that, okay? I don't want people to see me in the poop-mobile anymore."

Danny gasped. He really, actually gasped for the first time in his life. He had read in stories about people gasping, but hadn't thought it was really true. The *poop-mobile*. How could Beau say that?

"So don't wait for me, okay?" said Beau.

Danny spent days thinking about this, with the terrible feeling of a hole in his stomach. He didn't ever want his mother, or especially his father, to learn what Beau had said. But he wanted just as badly to tell *someone*, as though the name was trying to get out from inside him, like the words he had written on a matchbook.

So he told a dog; it made sense to him. He told the nearest dog, the only one in the Hollow.

It belonged to Mrs. Elliot, who lived in the oldest house, and was so old herself that Danny imagined the great cottonwood trees had only been saplings when she'd arrived. She had told him once, with a smile that was both shy and horrible, that she had carved her initials on one of them when she was very young, and Danny imagined that he would have to climb to the very tip of the tree—a hundred feet up—to find where her letters had grown to. She was always pleased when he came to play with her dog, a tiny thing she called Josephine. Danny thought it was the ugliest dog in the city, like a shaved rat with half its tail cut off, but he'd grown quite fond of it, and knew that Josephine thought of herself as a big and beautiful poodle. He was glad that dogs didn't really understand mirrors.

Josephine had listened to many of his problems, from the time when he was four and he was frightened to tell his mother that he'd lost his mittens again. Now he explained about Beau and the poop-mobile as they played in Mrs.

Elliot's yard. The dog sat and listened, with her little rat face all screwed up in thought; then she leapt up and licked his nose, and Danny knew she'd understood.

"Yeah, it'll be okay," he said. "It just bothered me, you know." He stretched out on his back, and Josephine bounced on his chest, trying to lick his eyes as Danny wriggled and laughed.

Mrs. Elliot came out and watched, sitting on the back steps with her dress bundled up to her gray knees. "You're a sweetheart to play with her, Danny," she said. "When I pass on, I think she should go to you."

Danny said, "Well, thanks, Mrs. Elliot. But I'm going to have a dog of my own pretty soon. I just know it."

nineteen

Danny dreamed he was standing on a beach with Beau, on a sandy beach in a crimson twilight. He and Beau were standing side by side; then suddenly Beau was floating in the air, and he had turned into a little satellite, a metal ball with spikes and stalks. He hovered there, beeping shrill Morse code, flashing red lights from the stalks. In the dream, Danny tried to understand what Beau was saying, but couldn't. Then Beau—satellite Beau—went zooming to the horizon, shrinking to a speck in a second, before he was gone altogether.

It was the most troubling dream that Danny had ever dreamt, for he saw its meaning very clearly. He was losing Beau. His brother would change, and soon leave him behind.

Because the signs had come in a dream, Danny believed

this had to be true. It was hard for him, though, because he couldn't *see* any difference. On school nights, Danny lay on his bed while Beau lay on his, doing his homework or working on his models. They watched TV from eight to nine. And every Sunday they went off to the fort they'd built in the woods, and sat in there talking about all sorts of things, but mostly of rocket ships and dogs, and sometimes of both at once.

"When you get a dog you should call it Rocket," said Beau one day, as they sat in the dark of the fort. "That's what I'd call a dog."

"Rocket," Danny echoed. Then he shouted, "Rocket!" and smiled. "Yeah, that's not bad. But I'm thinking of Texas. Or Billy Bear; I can't decide."

They were leaning against the back wall, and the roof was sagging above them. Outside, the leaves were turning yellow and red; they were gathering on the ground.

"Hey, I got a great name," said Beau.

"What?"

Beau moved his hands as he said it: "Laika."

Danny laughed. "No way, man."

"Come on, what's wrong with Laika?" Beau asked. "That's the best one yet. Laika the space dog. You know? The Russian space dog?"

"No way, man."

"Yes, way. Come on, Danny. You know what it means in Russian?" Beau didn't wait for an answer. "Barker, that's what. So you could call your dog Barker."

"Barker. Old Barker," said Danny. "I guess that's kinda

neat." He watched a beetle crawling across the floor. "It's like Old Yeller, 'cept he's barking instead of yelling."

"You dope," grunted Beau. "They didn't call him Old Yeller 'cause he yelled. He was a yellow dog. He was Old *Yellow*."

"No fooling?" asked Danny. "Man, you know everything, Beau."

Beau shrugged modestly.

"I wish you didn't have to be changing," said Danny. "What's going to happen, I wish it didn't have to."

"What do you mean?" asked Beau, making it sound like one long word, *whadayamean*. "What's going to happen?"

"I don't know." Danny saw the beetle bump up against the wall. It tried to climb it, then toppled backward and went off the way it had come. "I don't think you're going to hang around with me, you know, after a while."

"Aw, Danny," said Beau. "Sure I will."

"No matter what?"

"No matter what," said Beau. "I'll always hang around with you, Danny. I promise."

twenty

On Halloween they went together trick-or-treating. It was a Saturday night. Danny was a pirate with a wooden sword, a black bandanna, a patch on his eye. Beau dipped a pair of gloves and a set of the Old Man's coveralls into aluminum paint and turned himself into an astronaut. On his head he wore a bucket with a cutout for his face. But the bucket was far too big, and he stood in front of the mirror and said, "Oh, man. I look like Charlie Brown with a bucket on his head." At half the houses they stopped at that night people laughed out loud to see him. Old Mrs. Elliot, who wore her spectacles on a string, held them to her eyes and asked, "Are you pretending to be a good robot or a nasty robot?"

They worked their way through the Hollow, then along the streets toward the school. Danny's eye patch and bandanna fooled the people he knew, but not the dogs. They came bounding to meet him as they always had, and he fed them treats along the way, first the gooey marshmallow squares of Rice Krispies, then the pathetic little bags of popcorn that he wouldn't have eaten anyway.

It was cold that night. They could see frost on the grass and their breath in the air. Danny blew puffs from his mouth, then ran forward and tried to swallow them. They walked in a loop above the Hollow, not wanting to go down through the woods in the dark. Danny had heard that kids had been murdered in the woods, and he never went there after sunset. So they kept to the roads, then crossed the big bridge and went down to the Hollow. Beau took off his bucket and carried it under his arm.

There were no streetlights in the Hollow, and the woods along the creek were black and spooky. The jack-o'-lanterns seemed brighter there than anywhere else, staring from the porches with their fiery eyes and jagged grins. The street was empty, though from the heights above came faint cries of "Trick or treat!" and "Halloween aaapples!" Josephine yapped as they hurried past Mrs. Elliot's place.

As they reached their own house, the River boys saw the mountain of dirt from the Old Man's pit. It was enormous now, with the digging almost finished. The Old Man had been squaring the sides and laying metal bars for his concrete.

When Danny saw the pumper truck he nearly cried out. Its whole front was splattered again with eggs. Yolks and whites, half frozen by the frost, hung in dripping icicles from the grille and the bumper. He tugged at Beau's arm and got him to look. "I bet Creepy did that," he said.

"Yeah," said Beau.

The kitchen light was on, and they saw their mother at the sink, behind her row of dolls. It was strange to look in at her, knowing she couldn't look out. Danny wondered if Creepy had stood here doing the same thing as he held his carton of eggs. Then he peered into the darkness, trying to see over the edge and into the pit. "You don't think he's still here, do you?" he said.

"No, he's a bag of wind, like the Old Man says," said Beau. "He woulda buzzed off before anyone seen him."

"We should get him back," said Danny. "Let's get some soap and do his windows."

But Beau had a better idea. He filled his bucket from the septic truck, right to the edge of his cutout hole. He and Danny held their noses as the stuff came plopping and gurgling from the dumper valve. Then they carried it together, slung between them on Danny's pirate sword. They sloshed and staggered up the street to the Colvig house, one boy in a black bandanna and an eye patch, the other in an aluminum suit that shone with the faint fires of the jack-o'-lanterns.

The living room was brightly lit, the curtains drawn to all but a crack in the middle. They could see the flicker of the television set, and a big round shadow on the curtains, cast by what must have been either a pumpkin or Dopey's head.

They set the bucket on the driveway and cracked open

the door of Creepy Colvig's station wagon. The light came on inside. It glared on Beau's aluminum suit and on the whiteness of the bucket. To Danny it seemed shockingly bright, and he pulled away. "Let's forget it, Beau," he whispered. "Come on, he's going to see us."

"Watch the house," said Beau.

Danny stood with his wooden sword, watching the window. He heard the car's door creak. He heard the bucket bend as his brother picked it up. A great waft of the stench came over him, and he heard the slosh and splash, and the slam of the door.

"Let's get out of here," said Beau.

The streets were now empty except for the River boys. Even the jack-o'-lanterns had vanished—their candles burnt out—as though they'd tired of the night and fallen asleep. Beau was swinging the bucket as he ran, and both he and Danny were giggling about what they had done.

They were nearly home when Beau stopped in the middle of the street and held up the bucket. "What do I with this?" he said. "It's the Old Man's; I gotta clean it, Danny."

"Use the hose," said Danny.

But Beau said that was no good. "He'll hear the water running, Danny." He said they had no choice but to go down to the creek, down in the dark with no flashlight or anything, into the woods where Danny had heard that people had been murdered.

They chose the place where the bushes were thinnest, but still it was dark in there, as black as a vampire's cape. Danny thought he would maybe stand guard at the edge of the woods, but it seemed more frightening to be alone. So he followed Beau through the bushes, keeping so close to the silvery shimmer of the overalls that he bumped into them twice. They startled a cat, which startled them worse.

Beau rinsed the bucket in the stream while Danny stared all around, twisting his head as far as it could go, then back the other way. In his aluminum suit, Beau was like a ghost— just a shape only vaguely like a person. Danny kept wishing he was home, that they had never gone to Creepy's place.

"Aw, geez," said Beau.

"What's the matter?" asked Danny. He saw the silvery shadows of Beau's hands fly off from his arms, as though they'd been suddenly chopped away. He saw them land beside the creek, and felt almost like screaming.

"I got stuff on my gloves," said Beau. "Man, it stinks."

He buried the gloves in the soft black bed of Highland Creek. Then the boys crawled through the bushes, made their way to the street, and back to the house. They collected their bags of candy.

The Old Man was waiting at the door. He opened it as Danny was reaching for the handle, and looked down and said, "Come in."

Danny was sure right away that the Old Man knew what they'd done. But their mother came running to the door, saying, "Where have you been? I was worried sick about you."

"We went round by the school," said Danny. "We went right round the Hollow. Look what we got!" He tried to open his bag, but the Old Man plucked it from his hands.

"Why, the pair of you are soaking wet," said Mrs. River. "It's cold out there, and you're wet and—Beau, where are your gloves?"

Beau looked at his hands as though he had never noticed them before. "Maybe I didn't have any," he said.

"And maybe you did. I'm sure that you did." She seemed more worried than angry, but the Old Man was stern and tight-lipped, and that was what frightened Danny. It frightened him so much that he suddenly felt quite sick. He said, "Dad, someone egged the truck. It was probably Creepy Colvig and—"

"I know all about it," said the Old Man. "I know everything that happened to that truck tonight."

Danny turned pale. "Mom, I don't feel too good," he cried.

"Well, you've probably been stuffing yourself with candy," she told him.

"Or mixed up in some mischief," said the Old Man. "That's what *I* think, and you know why?"

Danny's voice had a tremble in it. "Because there's no secrets from the septic man?"

It seemed that the Old Man would either laugh or explode. For a moment he stood looking down with his lips trembling. Then he started to speak, and stopped and started again. "Well, there is that. But we were worried enough that we called Mrs. Parker to ask if she'd seen you at that end of the Hollow, and she looked out and said you were passing right then. She could see those aluminum clothes of yours, Beau."

"That was a good *twenty minutes* ago," said Mrs. River.

"Or more," said the Old Man. "I just don't understand how two boys can take half an hour to go half a block. But I'll tell you, I'm sure glad you're home."

So Danny learned that night that secrets *could* be kept from a septic man. On Sunday morning, as he and Beau sat in bed eating jelly beans and peanuts and tiny Hershey bars, covering their blankets with shells and wrappers, they heard a howl from up the street. It was a low-pitched, furious shout.

Danny looked at Beau, and Beau looked at him, but neither said a word.

Then Danny cracked another peanut.

twenty-one

The Old Man began pouring concrete in November. He mixed it up a batch at a time in big buckets that he'd been hoarding since September. But when the time came for his first pour, he found that he was one bucket short. It took him only a moment to realize that Beau had worn it on Halloween, and that was fine with him. But he had to find another, and the delay set him back by two days.

He poured only six inches of concrete before the coming winter caught him up. His lengths of reinforcing bar twisted in and out of the concrete like enormous worms, holding their spiky heads and tails a foot or so above the ground. Then the snow began to fall, and it capped his mountain first, then covered his metal worms. And on the last weekend of the month, the Old Man came into the house and threw down his cap. "I'm going to shut 'er down," he announced. "I'm finished till the spring."

It looked like a long and snowy winter, bound to be a white Christmas. This pleased the River boys, but Danny especially. There would be ice to smash on the pools of Highland Creek, and good sledding on Killer Hill, where a kid could coast from the top of the Hollow right into the tangle of trees.

In December, when Danny was on his third pair of mittens, he began to worry less about his strange vision of Beau as a satellite. His dreams were never wrong, but there had been no terrible change. With football finished, he was seeing even more of his brother than he had before. He worried instead about Christmas. It was coming quickly, but he had no feeling yet that he would be given a dog on Christmas morning.

He started scheming for that in the middle of the month. He drew outlines of dogs in the mist that formed on the kitchen window. Instead of snowmen he built snowdogs, and dragged his mother out to see them.

School finished on the seventeenth. As usual, Beau had done well, and Danny rather poorly. *Danny is a pleasure in the classroom*, his teacher had written in the report. *But I wish he would apply himself harder*. The Old Man, after reading that, said he should apply his hand to Danny's backside, but of course he never did. He only offered to reward them both by taking them to the A&W. Danny said he would like that, but Beau said he was "kinda busy."

The next day Danny followed his mother all over the house on his hands and knees, pretending to be a dog. He scraped at the back of her leg with his fingernails; he sat up and begged for his breakfast, then ate his cereal on the floor, lapping it from the bowl. He barked for more, until his mother finally said, "Great balls of fire, Danny. If you keep this up, they won't know whether to put you in the nut-house or the kennel."

On the nineteenth, she took Danny into the city so that he could do his shopping. He sat on the knees of nine different Santas, one in each place that they went to, telling each one the same thing—in a voice loud enough for his mother to hear—that he wanted a puppy for Christmas. He plunked himself down and bellowed in their ears. He knew, of course, that they were just men in red suits, but he was still disappointed to have a Santa Claus tell him, "Pipe down, will ya!"

The tree went up on the twenty-first, and then the presents began to appear. Danny took them one by one in his hands, squeezing and shaking and sniffing, hoping to find a collar and leash, or a food bowl, or a squeaky toy. On Christmas Eve he discovered a big box that rattled when he shook it, and he was certain it was full of puppy food.

That afternoon the Old Man filled a big jug with water. He poured some into the tree stand, then left the jug nearby, and Danny's heart took a little jump, because he knew what *that* was for. He tried to pretend that he didn't, so as not to spoil the Old Man's pleasure, but couldn't stop himself from asking. "Why are you leaving the water there?" he said, so excited he could hardly talk.

"Why lug it back and forth?" said the Old Man. "There'll be a need for it tomorrow, I'm sure."

That was all Danny needed to know. His heart filled with joy, and he went out in the snow, to Killer Hill, to watch the dogs chasing sleds and snowballs. For a moment he wished, with sadness, that he hadn't lost Billy Bear's name tag. But he was too happy to stay sad for long, and all evening he wondered how the puppy would be presented to him. He hoped it would be lying on his bed in the morning, nestled in the bend of his knee, or pressed against his neck, and that it would wake him with little nips and kisses, with its tiny tail wagging furiously. Or, he wondered, would he find it tied to the tree by a red ribbon, and would it leap forward to meet him when he came into the room, tugging so hard at the ribbon that the tree would shake and the ornaments tremble? Or would it be waiting outside, out in the truck, so that he wouldn't hear it barking? No matter how it would happen, he would take his puppy for a walk right away, and he would have to beat a trail through the snow to let it follow behind him. Just before bedtime, he placed his boots by the register in the mudroom so that they would be toasty in the morning.

Old Man River followed the boys to their room. He had to duck his head as he passed below the airplanes and the rockets that dangled from the ceiling on Beau's side. Then he sat on Beau's bed and opened a book, and read "The Night Before Christmas," as he did every year. With the last sentence, "A merry Christmas to all, and to all a good night," he closed the book softly. He tucked the boys in tightly and kissed them good night.

Danny thought he wouldn't sleep at all. He lay awake, staring at the patterns of frost on the window, as names of dogs went racing through his mind. Every one he'd thought of, and every one he'd forgotten, came to him in a great rush, like a babble of shouting. There were others now, too, all Christmasy things like Sugarplum and Marzipan, and the swirl of names seemed to sweep him along into darkness.

But there was no puppy on his bed in the morning. There was no puppy tied to the tree, and no one told him to go out and look in the truck. He opened the box that he'd thought was dog food and found it was only a Crazy Clock game, with all its plastic pieces rattling. One after the other, he tore open his presents and put them aside. No leash. No squeaky toys. No dog food bowl. Beside him, Beau was shrieking at his finds—a bank like a Mercury space capsule, a Jupiter four-color signal gun, and a big Rocket Base USA. He fired one of its missiles and hit Danny in the back of the head.

Danny didn't even move. He was so disappointed that he just sat and stared at the boxes and the wrapping paper. He kept hoping that somehow a puppy would appear, but it never did. He would have sat there and cried if he hadn't known how much it would hurt his parents' feelings to see him do that on Christmas. So he played with his Jumbo the Bubble-Blowing Elephant, and let Beau shoot missiles at the bubbles it made. And he played with his Agent M Radio Rifle, and bounced his Superball, and hoped he would get his dog in 1965.

twenty-two

The sheriff grew bored with standing in the doorway. He tugged at his belt and shifted his feet. In the cell, the lady kept talking.

The blond-haired boy watched her closely. She reminded him a lot of his mother, with her old-fashioned clothes and the golden band on her finger. Her voice was like his mother's Scarlett voice, all bright and chirpy, rising often into questions that weren't really questions at all.

She told him about the little town and the people who lived there. Then he asked if she'd been to Cape Canaveral, and she said, "Just once," so he made her tell him all about it. She said she'd toured the space center. "I got a little ol' book from there?" she said, like a question.

"Did you meet any astronauts?"

"Not real ones, no. But I got my picture taken with a cardboard astronaut," she said.

"I want to go there," said the boy. "That's where I was trying to get to."

"Oh? Why's that?" she said.

"I can't tell you," said the boy. "I would, but you'd laugh at me."

"Now why would I do something like that?" she said.

"Because no one believes me," said the boy.

twenty-three

In the spring of 1965, as the snow was melting, Mrs. River was longing for summer and her trip to Georgia. It was spring as well in the novel she was writing, and as she looked out the kitchen window she felt as though she was in her story, gazing at plantations battered by the guns of the Civil War.

It was a Tuesday in March, but she wasn't writing today because both the boys were home from school. Beau had space fever again, and Danny had caught a dose of it. They were watching TV in the living room, waiting for the launch of Gemini 3. She heard Beau shout.

"There he is! Look, Danny!" he said, in that voice that hadn't quite broken. "Aw, Danny, aren't you watching?"

"Sure I am," said Danny. "It was Gus Grisson. I seen him."

Mrs. River raised her voice and called through the house, "You *saw* him."

"He didn't! He wasn't even watching," answered Beau.

She took one more look at her dolls, then went into the living room. Beau was sitting on the floor, cross-legged like a snake charmer, and Danny was sprawled in the armchair. On the television screen, two astronauts were squeezing into a little elevator. She watched them come out at the top of the rocket and climb one after the other into the capsule. "What a tiny door," she said. They had to go through it feet-first, with men in white coats trying to help. "Couldn't they give them a bigger door than that?"

"It's a hatch," said Beau. "It has to be small."

"And this is what *you* want to do someday?" she asked.

"It's not just what I *want*," said Beau. "I'm really going to do it, Mom."

"It looks so dangerous," she said. "You'd rather fly in rockets than be a doctor or a lawyer?"

"Or a septic man?" asked Danny.

Beau didn't look away from the television. "There's nothing else I wanta do. I'm gonna fly in a fighter jet. And I'm gonna float around in space. You'll see."

"Well, don't ask me to go down and watch you blast off," she said. "I'll be sitting right here crossing my fingers and crossing my toes and—"

"Shhh!" said Beau. "Mom, please, I can't hear."

Mrs. River didn't mean to sit and watch the launch, but she did. She found that she couldn't walk away from the television, and so she settled like a bird on the arm of the sofa. The countdown was going on as the astronauts vanished into that capsule. She saw one of the white-coated men reach through the hatch, and the hand of an astronaut come up to shake his. It amazed her that this was really happening at this very moment, hundreds of miles away. Even as she watched, the astronaut was squeezing the hand of the man in the coat, and the man was squeezing back, and they both knew that in minutes the astronaut would be riding a rocket through space. Then the door was closed and latched, and the men in white coats went down in the elevator. *And the poor astronauts*, thought Mrs. River. *The poor astronauts, they must be feeling so lonely.*

"Aren't they scared?" she asked.

"Only Gus," said Danny, in his armchair.

Beau became instantly furious. He turned and screamed at his brother. "You *shut up!*" He actually *screamed*, and his face was purple, and his eyes were bulging like a devil's. She had never seem him so angry at anything, and over two words? "Beau!" she said.

Danny looked stunned. "Gee, I was only fooling."

"Well, don't!" shouted Beau. "You little moron. Get outta here, Danny."

"Now, Beau," said Mrs. River. "Just whoa, Beau."

That was how she had calmed him ever since he was a baby. For thirteen years it had made him slow down, and then stop, and then smile. But now it didn't work at all. He leapt up and wrestled Danny from the armchair, and Danny shouted, and she had to pry them apart.

"What's the matter?" she said. "What's the *matter* with you?"

"Take it back!" said Beau to Danny. "Gus Grissom isn't scared. He's never scared. You got no right to say it."

"Well, he certainly didn't seem frightened to me," said Mrs. River. "Oh, look. There's the rocket standing there now and—see?—that thing is moving away."

The boys only glared at each other.

"You're stupid, Danny. You don't know anything about him," said Beau. "He was a colonel in the air force. He flew a hundred missions in Korea. He's a hero, and he doesn't get scared."

"Okay," said Mrs. River. "Okay, we've settled that. Danny said he was only joking."

"Then it was a stupid joke," said Beau.

"Maybe it was," she said. "But if you don't sit down and watch, you're going to miss the launch."

Beau turned away. He lay on his stomach and made blinkers from his hands, as though to block out all but the TV. Danny got back in his chair. He sulked for a while; then he said, "I'm sorry, Beau. I didn't mean nothing."

"Forget it," said Beau.

"He's the bravest guy in the world. I know it," said Danny.

"Just forget it, okay?"

"In a minute he'll be the bravest guy in space, too. He'll be the bravest guy in the whole universe."

"Okay!" shouted Beau. But then he shook his head and rolled his eyes, and didn't look angry anymore. Mrs. River sighed happily. The boys hardly ever fought, and they *never* stayed angry for long.

All three of them counted out the last seconds to the launch, and all three leaned forward as flames shot from the base of the rocket, then clouds of smoke billowed in rolls. They gasped as the rocket started up—so incredibly slowly—and cheered as it went faster and faster. They could hear Gus Grissom talking on the radio, just as coolly and calmly as if he was sitting there with them, watching on TV.

A camera was trying to follow the rocket, and the little white streak that was all they could see flickered and bounced across the screen. There was a sudden puff of smoke around it, and Mrs. River cried out, "Oh, no! What's wrong?"

"Nothing," said Beau. "That was the first stage separating."

A man on the TV said the same thing a second later. Then Gus Grissom's calm voice remarked on the shock, and the rocket went higher and higher.

"Could we see it?" asked Danny. "If we went outside, could we see it?"

"Nah, not from here."

"How high up are they now?"

Beau didn't answer.

"How high, Beau?" asked Danny.

He still said nothing. Mrs. River said, "Danny, he probably doesn't know." But then Beau said, "Seven miles," and his voice was a bit hoarse. He said, "Now ten. Now twenty. They see the sky getting darker, and the stars coming out in the day. Now they see the world like a ball, and they keep going up and . . ."

"And what?" asked Danny, after a moment. "And what, Beau?"

Beau shook his head. He was crying, Mrs. River could tell. Or maybe not really crying, but *awed* by what he was seeing. The sight of a rocket going into space had struck him so deeply that he couldn't even talk. Right then, Mrs. River decided that she wouldn't try to stop him, not ever, no matter what he wanted to do.

Gemini 3 was halfway to Russia already. Gus Grissom and John Young would fly the capsule three times around the world. They would share a corned-beef sandwich that Young had smuggled aboard, and scramble to catch the crumbs floating weightless all around them. They would see the sun rise and set in an hour, and look down on half of the USA in a glance. Then they'd ride the thing to Earth in a fireball.

It would be four hours, fifty-two minutes, and thirty-one seconds between liftoff and splashdown. There would be news reports, and bits of film broadcast as soon as they were rushed in and developed. Beau spent nearly every moment in front of the TV. He got up only once, to fetch a pen and a sheet of paper, so that he could write a letter to Gus Grissom.

Dear Mr. Grissom,

Congratulations on being the first guy to go twice into space. You haven't landed yet, but I know that you will and that you will NOT have the same troubles as last time in Liberty Bell 7! (Like your hatch blowing off and your capsule sinking.) I know you weren't scared the first time. I laughed when I heard how you named this capsule Molly Brown, for that lady who couldn't sink.

Someday I'm going to be an astronaut too. I'm going to go into the air force like you did and I hope there is a war somewhere so that I can fly a hundred combat missions like you did. My dad says there might be a war in Vietnam and that's why he is building a shelter in our front yard, but I would be happy.

We are going to drive to Cape Canaveral this summer to see the launch of Gemini 4 or maybe Gemini 5. If you could take a minute to meet us that would be really great. But I know you might be busy with astronaut stuff.

Well, that's all. You're going to be landing soon and I don't want to miss it. GOOD LUCK!!!!! Don't blow it. (Ha, ha!)
Your great friend,
Beau River

twenty-four

There was a problem with Gemini 3. It came down too soon and too fast, and Mrs. River and her boys sat fretting. They didn't hear the great splash of the capsule hitting the water, or the crack as Gus Grissom's helmet split across the faceplate. They didn't hear the surprise in the men's voices, but knew the capsule was beyond the reach of the rescue ships. They worried as the helicopters flew off to find it.

"I hope those men are all right," said Mrs. River. "I hope they're okay."

When they saw the film, with the capsule floating on its side, Beau thought something was wrong. "It should be sitting up," he said.

But a man on TV said everything looked "A-OK." He said the Gemini capsules were meant to float sideways like tipped-over corks. Then the helicopters dropped lower, and divers tumbled into the water with their frogmen suits and fins. They swam to the capsule, and the hatch swung open, and Gus Grissom came through it, waving.

Mrs. River and the boys stood up and cheered.

By the time the Old Man came home, the mission was over, and the boys were out playing. Mrs. River gave him the letter that Beau had written, and she watched as he read it.

"I've never seen a boy so passionate about anything," she said. "Charlie, when the rocket went up he was crying. He didn't want anyone to know, but he was. He was weeping, Charlie."

The Old Man stood there in his coveralls, the letter in one hand, his cap in the other. It took him so long to answer that he must have read the letter two or three times. Then he gave it back and turned toward the window, squinting out at his great mountain of dirt.

"No son of mine's going into the air force," he said. "I won't let him bomb peasants in the fields. Looking forward to war? I'll show him what war's all about."

"Oh, great balls of fire!" said Mrs. River. "Didn't you see what he's saying, Charlie? It's not about going to war."

But the Old Man quoted from the letter, word for word: *I hope there is a war somewhere.* "Well, he'll get his wish. It's coming to that."

"Oh, I knew I shouldn't have shown you this," she said. "I was hoping you would—" She stopped and looked up at him. "It's not the war, is it?" she asked. "That's not what you care about. Charlie, you're jealous."

"Huh. *Jealous*," he said, and laughed.

"You are. You're afraid he thinks more of Gus Grissom than he does of you. *You* want to be his only hero. Well, Charlie, for heaven's sake—"

"That's crazy," he said. "Do you even know what's happening in Vietnam now? Do you know how much it's changed since I started digging out there? There's B-52s blasting the country. Operation *Rolling Thunder*! It's Operation Kill Peasants in Rice Fields. It's Operation Drag Us into War, that's what it is."

He picked up his cap and went out. Mrs. River saw him through the window, scaling his mountain for the first time that spring. With the coming of winter he had put layers of plastic in and around the hole, and now he started pulling them away.

She went out after him, in her slippers and dress, in her hillbilly clothes, shouting at him, "Don't walk away! Tarnation!"

They shouted back and forth, up and down, from the hill of mud to the bottom of the pit. The Old Man was standing among his reinforcing bars, tearing the plastic sheets from the rusting, poking-up ends of metal. He looked like a tiger in a tiger trap.

"Do you think you can hide him down in that hole?" she shouted. "Do you think you can put him in a box and seal him off from the world? He's going to grow up, you know, Charlie. He's going to do what he wants."

"He's too young to *know* what he wants," the Old Man shouted back.

"Don't you dare try to spoil his dreams," she said.

He was wrestling with the plastic, pulling long shreds through the metal spikes. When he had it all free, he tried to hurl it from the pit in a huge ball. But it only rolled back down on top of him.

"Charlie," she said.

"I'm not going to spoil his dreams," he said. "I just want him to grow up and have a chance to live them. Is that so bad?"

He grabbed one end of the plastic and climbed from the pit, dragging it all behind him. He climbed right past Flo, over the top, and down the other side. The plastic rippled and snaked behind him.

" 'Give up the stars, Beau.' Is that what you'll tell him?" she asked. " 'Keep your feet on the ground and your head in the dirt.' " She glared at him as he came back. "What about the trip to the Cape? I suppose you'll tell him to forget it now."

He grimaced at that—*the Cape*—as if they were all talking like astronauts now. "No, that's more important than ever," he said. "I want him to see the rockets and all, and ache to get into space. Then I'll tell him that he doesn't have to join the air force to do it. There'll be scientists in space by the time he's ready, and plumbers and doctors, if there's still a world to launch them from. And if there's not, well, the four of us will be here in the shelter, waiting it out. I'm covering all the bases, Flo."

"You don't have to tell him anything," she said. "Charlie, please. Just let him grow up on his own. Let him find out those things himself. I wish you'd fill in that hole and let him grow up."

twenty-five

Toward the end of March it started to rain, and the rain kept up for weeks. The Old Man's mountain eroded into gulleys and crags. Brown glaciers flowed from the top, creeping toward the pit. Mrs. River hoped the whole thing would collapse into itself, hiding forever the terrible future that hole represented.

She had told the boys not to play there but knew they did. For Danny especially, it was irresistible, the mud perfect for shaping into river canyons and underground streams. He'd leveled out a lake near the summit and directed its runoff in every direction. The mountain was riddled with his bits of pipe, waterways, and spidery bridges.

He spent hours building elaborate castles that clung to the cliffs, then knocked them down with mud bombs. Beau would join him for that, the pair of them yelling as their bombs burst and the castles crumbled.

In the middle of April the Old Man got angry about it. Mrs. River heard him drive up in the truck and, looking out, saw him staring into the hole. Then he waded through the mud and came in, and he threw down his cap and said, "For crying out loud, can't you keep an eye on those boys?"

"Well, hello to you, too," she said.

"I can't keep up with them," he said. "I spend every night just shoveling out the dirt they've pushed in during the day. You can't pour concrete onto dirt, Flo. I'll never get finished at this rate."

"Tell them yourself to stay away," she said, rather coldly.

"I've told them until I'm blue in the face," said Old Man River. "I'm not here to watch them, but you are. Is it too much to ask that you keep them out of the dirt? Is that too much for you, Flo?"

He marched off to change his septic-pumping coveralls for his mud-digging coveralls. As he passed her again he said, "Sometimes I don't know why I bother. There I am, breaking my back for you and the boys, and what do I get? Nothing."

He slammed the door behind him and went angrily into his hole, and after that she didn't bother much with the boys. If they wanted to fill in the pit with their mud bombs and castles, that was fine with her.

In the last week of April she was in the basement when she heard them at the game. She was writing away in her notebook, scribbling quickly. She was on Chapter 83 and her heroine, Cherry O'Day, was about to slap the daylights out of a meddlesome Yankee.

She tried to ignore the shouts of the boys. But Danny's voice came piercing through the walls, and she heard him yell, "Fire one! Fire two!"

Mrs. River trudged up the stairs and looked out the window. Beau was firing the little rockets from his Christmas toy, and Danny was the target. He was dashing across the mountain, and both of them were laughing. She tapped on the window and caught their attention, then shook her finger and mouthed, "You be careful."

Back she went to the basement. She read what she'd written, and started midsentence. . . . *damned Yankee!" screamed Cherry O'Day. Her bosom was heaving.* Flo's pencil scratched over the paper.

From outside, through the walls and through the floor, came Danny's voice again, now angry. "Get out of here! Buzz off, will you!"

She imagined that Beau had finally hit him with one of the little rockets. So she got up and turned on the washing machine. Its rush of water hid the sounds, and she filled the page and turned to the next. *Cherry O'Day was a red-headed polecat.*

She wrote and wrote, seeing it all in her mind, the carpetbagger holding up his arms as Cherry flew at him with her bodice ripped open. She didn't hear the whirls and thumps of the washing machine, or the rattle of her chair;

she didn't hear anything but the *slap-slap-slap* of Cherry's hands, and Cherry's voice shouting out, "You vahmint! You Yankee!" She saw Cherry wild-eyed, her clothes flapping like flags, her buttoned boots kicking.

Then it all faded away.

Danny was screaming.

twenty-six

Mrs. River took the stairs three at a time, flying up from the basement, out through the house.

She saw Danny standing on the mountain, bashing his own cheeks with his fists. "Beau!" he cried. *"Beau!"*

She ran up toward him, shouting his name, but he didn't seem to hear. Her feet sank into the mud, and one of her slippers came away, and then the other one. Twice she fell and caught herself, until her hands were black to the wrists and her fingers were like sausages of mud. "Danny!" she shrieked as she raced up the mountain. "Danny, what's wrong?"

He fell to his knees, still hitting himself. He kept shouting, but nothing she could understand.

As she came up beside him and looked, she spotted Beau at the bottom of the pit, Beau lying all crooked on the concrete, lying in the rain and the mud. Her first thought was that the puddle of water was the color of peach blossoms. Then she saw that Beau had fallen onto one of the reinforcing bars, and that it had pierced right through his chest.

"Get up!" she shouted at him. "Get up right now and don't try to frighten me."

But Beau did not get up. He didn't move. His eyes were partly open, his fingers curled nearly into fists. There was a rip in his shirt, and blood was seeping from his mouth.

Mrs. River dropped to her knees. She grabbed Danny. She pulled him against her, and she felt him go all loose, like a bit of old rope. Then she screamed and screamed and screamed, until someone came to help her.

It was Mrs. Elliot from up the street. She came running in her old-lady shoes, her spectacles swinging on the string round her neck. She tried to climb the mountain but couldn't. All covered in mud, she stood at the bottom and shouted up, "What's happened, Flo? What on earth has happened?"

When a car came by, she ran and flagged it down— Creepy Colvig in his station wagon. He swerved right past the old woman before he stopped. Then his brake lights flashed red, and Mrs. Elliot screamed at him, "You get out of that car! You come here and help!"

He scaled the mountain. He took one look in the pit, then led Mrs. River and Danny down to the road.

twenty-seven

An ambulance came, its lights flashing, its siren whooping through the Hollow. Men in blue jackets went into the pit, and they fussed over Beau, but didn't bring him out. They put a blanket right over him, right over his face, until only his fingers were poking out.

The police came next. They came in two cars, the lights going round and round on their roofs, and the policemen looked in the pit but didn't bother going down. They took out black notebooks and skinny little pens. They talked to Danny and Mrs. River. They asked Danny, "Can you tell us what happened, son?"

Danny said he couldn't remember what happened. A policeman said, "You're not in trouble, son. No one's going to get angry with you."

Then Danny said he did remember. He said, "Dopey was here. Dopey came and pushed him."

"That's the Colvig boy," said Mrs. River. She was holding Danny. "They live up the street."

The police went to the Colvig house, then came back and talked to Danny again. They said Mr. Colvig had told them his son hadn't left the house that morning. "Were you just playing?" asked one of the policemen. "Is that it? Were you just playing, and your brother had an accident?"

"I don't remember," said Danny. "I think it was Dopey."

The Old Man arrived half an hour later, roaring down the hill in the big truck, another police car in front of him with its siren blaring.

Everyone who lived in Hog's Hollow had gathered outside the gray house, and they all shuffled aside as Old Man River pulled up in the truck. A policeman got them to move away, and they retreated to the other side of the street.

The Old Man came out of the truck looking like a figure made of chalk. His boots slipped in the mud as he hurried to Flo, who stood with Danny at the foot of the steps. He hugged them both at once, and then he shook and trembled, and looked up at the sky with his face all wet with tears.

"What happened?" he asked.

"It was that pit," she said. "It was that goddamned hole of yours."

twenty-eight

For two hours Beau lay at the bottom of the pit, in the rain and the mud. Men in business suits took pictures of him, their flashbulbs popping out blasts of white light. Then the ambulance people zipped him into a black bag and carried him out.

The men in their suits asked all the same questions that the police had asked. They stayed all that day and came back the next, and the next after that. They knocked at every door along the winding street, and they plodded up and down through the pit until their black shoes were just blobs of thick mud. They talked to the Colvigs and talked to the Rivers. Again and again, they asked Danny what happened.

Danny stuck to his story. "We were playing," he said. "Then Dopey came, and I don't remember after that."

Whenever he tried to remember, it was like looking through a fog. Sometimes it was like looking into blackness, and he could never be sure what he really remembered and what he thought he remembered. "I think it was Dopey who pushed him," he said.

Creepy Colvig also came to the old gray house. Danny heard him shouting and, looking out, saw three men in suits holding him back. Creepy was like a big, raging bear, bellowing at them as he thrashed out with his arms. He was like a big bear trying to get into the house, and Danny—terrified that he would break loose from the men—hid trembling under the kitchen table.

That evening, the men in suits sat in Danny's living room. As the Old Man and Mrs. River watched, one of the men had his last talk with Danny. "Look," he said, "it's all up to you, son. If you say the Colvig boy pushed your brother, he'll be put away. Maybe for a long time. Now, are you sure that's what you want to happen, Danny? Are you absolutely sure about this?"

Danny started crying. He thought of Creepy shouting on the lawn, and saw him twice as big and twice as mean as ever, towering over the men in their suits. He imagined that if he said yes right now and Dopey was put away, Creepy would come back and kill him. He was sure of it. Creepy would find him one day in the Hollow, or come one night to his bedroom, and kill him for what he had said.

"Well, son?" asked the man. He was sitting on the sofa beside Danny, his arm on its back. His fingers, very lightly, touched Danny's shoulder. "It's all up to you. You're the only one who was there."

Through his tears, Danny looked at Flo and said, "Oh, Mom!"

The Old Man leapt up. "This has got to stop!" he shouted. "It's got to stop right now. My boy's dead; he's gone. Don't you think it's punishment enough for the other one?"

In a calm and quiet voice, the man in the suit answered. "It's one more question, sir. Just one last question." He turned again to Danny. "Did the Colvig boy push your brother?"

Danny slowly shook his head. "I don't remember," he said. "I don't remember what happened."

The men in the suits went away then, and didn't come back. It was decided that the cause of Beau's death was "undetermined."

In the Hollow, people thought that Danny was paying dearly for a terrible accident. Mrs. Elliot put her pale hand on top of Flo's and said, "I'm so sorry. Poor Danny must feel terrible."

Danny was there, and he didn't argue. He wasn't sure himself what had really happened anymore; it hardly felt real. He knew that Beau was dead, but he couldn't stop thinking that someone would come along at any moment and tell him that it hadn't happened at all, or shake him from a nightmare.

It felt that way through the funeral service, and the burial, and the horrible afternoon when people came to the house and ate sandwiches and smoked cigarettes and told him what a brave little boy he was.

His father made a phone call, and a yellow machine arrived. It pushed all the dirt into the pit, then trundled and clanked back and forth on its Caterpillar tracks. It smoothed the lawn to its old flatness, leaving the dirt pressed into long lines of little brown cakes.

Danny found no pleasure in watching the machine. He found no pleasure in anything.

It was terrible to lie in his bed at night and not have Beau there beside him. But it was worse to wake in the mornings and see that Beau's bed hadn't been touched, and to see the model rockets hanging from the ceiling, and Beau's schoolbooks on the chair, where Beau had put them down on his last Friday. It was terrible to sit at the breakfast table, and terrible to watch TV.

It was terrible to go back to school, and to have all the children look at him, all the teachers touch him. No one called him Polluto or Stinky River, but he almost wished they would. He took the big bridge there and back, trekking across the heights. More scared than ever that Dopey would find him, he never went along the trails.

There was not a moment he didn't think of Beau. Even asleep, he had Beau in his mind, and saw him in all sorts of dreams. He would dream that the front door opened, and there would be Beau. Or he would dream that he was outside, playing in the creek, and suddenly he would look up and see Beau walking down the path. Beau would smile and wave and call out, "Hey, Danny! I'm okay; look, I'm okay."

And sometimes Beau would seem just fine, and sometimes he would have an iron bar sticking out of his chest, but he wouldn't know it was there.

The house was so quiet that Danny could hardly stand it. He could sit in the living room with his parents and hear the cat clock in the kitchen shifting its eyes back and forth. They spent hours sitting there, with no one saying a word, his mother just sighing and sighing, the Old Man gazing at his hands. But, bad as *that* was, it was worse when his parents fought. Anything could set them off, and then they stood and screamed at each other, shouting about silly things like books put in the wrong places, or footprints on the floor. The one thing they never shouted about was Beau, but Danny had a feeling that it was all about Beau. He thought his parents blamed each other for what had happened, and blamed themselves as well. They never came right out and blamed Danny, but they barely talked to him.

On Sundays they went to the place where Beau was buried. They drove in Mrs. River's Pontiac, though the Old Man did the driving. Mrs. River took a bunch of flowers, and the Old Man took scissors so that he could cut the clumps of grass around the stone. He would snip and snip, then get up and wander away.

On the third Sunday, Danny took a rocket from Beau's Rocket Base USA and buried it in the dirt. He poked a hole with his finger, then wedged the rocket into the grass. He could feel its nose cone sticking out. He wondered if Beau could see it.

That day, on the way home, his parents talked to him for

the first time about what had happened. The Old Man started it. "Look, Danny boy," he said, "we're not blaming you." And Danny knew then that they were. "We're not blaming you at all," said the Old Man. "We just want to know what went on that day."

"Can you tell us?" asked his mother. "We just want to know what happened."

"I've told you," said Danny. "I was playing with Beau." It made him nearly dizzy to peer back through the fog and the blackness. "We were playing rockets," he said, "and Beau was trying to shoot me. Then Dopey came from nowhere."

The Old Man and Mrs. River turned their heads and frowned at each other, then turned away again.

"Danny, I didn't see the Colvig boy," said Mrs. River, facing straight ahead.

"Then he musta come after you looked," said Danny. "I think he wanted one of the rockets; that's why he came. But I wouldn't give it to him. He tried to push me in the pit. It was nearly *me* that fell in the pit."

"I don't remember that boy *ever* coming to play with you," said Mrs. River.

"He didn't come to *play*," said Danny. The big car carried them along in its quiet rumble. "But he did come before. He did. When Dad was digging, he came to look at the hole."

"Well, everyone came to look at that hole," said Mrs. River, fussing with her pocketbook. "No one could understand what *that* was about. Great balls of fire, neither could I."

twenty-nine

They drove down into Hog's Hollow and right past the house. Mrs. River said, "Where are you going?" but the Old Man didn't answer. He steered the big car round the bends in the street, then pulled into the driveway at the Colvig house.

"Stay here," he said, and got out.

Danny watched him climb up to the porch and knock on the door. He knocked three times, waited a moment, then knocked three times again. The curtains shivered in the narrow window beside the door, and then the door opened a bit and Creepy Colvig stood there in the darkness behind it.

The car was still running. The engine speeded up by itself, then slowed with a jingly sound like the Old Man's keys.

Creepy was talking. He was shaking his head and talking, but Danny couldn't hear what he was saying. The Old Man moved closer, and Creepy stuck out one of his thick, hairy arms.

"My boy had nothing to do with it!" shouted Creepy Colvig. "Can't you get it through your head? He wasn't there! I go to work, he looks after himself. He takes care of himself. My boy doesn't run wild like a goddamn savage."

The Old Man talked, and Creepy gestured with his hairy arm. He glared down at the car, right through the windshield and right at Danny. Then he tried to shut the door on the Old Man. "Get outta here, or I'll call the goddamn cops!" he shouted.

There was a bit of a scuffle, and the Old Man reared back as the door closed with a bang.

He walked down the steps and toward the car, and Danny saw that he had a bruise on his cheek. His lip was torn, and he kept dabbing the blood with his knuckles. "Drive home, Flo," he said, and walked right past the car.

He was halfway home before they overtook him, and he didn't even look up.

thirty

Danny went right to his room when he got home. He had taken it on himself to look after Beau's things, and he used one of his socks—from the pile on the floor—to brush away the dust that was settling on Beau's schoolbooks on the chair, and on Beau's Mercury bank on the bookcase, and on his model of a Titan rocket on the windowsill. He pulled the covers very tight on Beau's bed, so that he would be sure to see a dent in them if Beau somehow came back and lay there again.

His mother came in as he was standing on Beau's table, trying to reach up to the model T-38 that hung above it, so that he could dust the wings. He was stretching up as high as he could, and all the strings of the airplanes were tangled round his arm, when his mother suddenly shouted from the doorway, "Danny!"

She dragged him down from there and rubbed her hands all over his head and his back. "What were you doing? What were you thinking?" she said.

"I was cleaning the models," said Danny.

"Oh," she said. "Oh, Danny. I thought—" She sobbed and shook. "I thought you were trying to hang yourself."

She took him to the kitchen and made him toast with peanut butter. She cut the toast into fingers, the way he'd liked it when he was four years old. She put them on a yellow plate, arranged like spokes on a wheel. She got him orange juice and cookies from the big cookie jar that looked like a dog.

"Danny, you're the most precious thing in the world to me. To both of us," she said. "We can't go back to what we had. We can't ever go back, and we don't want to forget it. But maybe we can put it behind us now and just carry on somehow. Just carry on."

Things were better after that. It seemed to Danny that all of them had fallen into the pit together, and that the yellow machine had covered them over and locked them inside it. And now, except for Beau, they were coming out again, crawling up through the mud. The Old Man wasn't as quick to change as Danny's mother was, but slowly he did, like a snowman melting. Then the three of them began to talk about Beau, and that pleased Danny enormously, because it had seemed that his parents were trying to forget him. Sometimes they even laughed at things that Beau had done.

They began by talking of things long ago, and then more

recent, and nearly right to the day that Beau "had his accident." But they never, ever talked about the accident itself.

The days went by. Danny kept trekking to school over the big bridge and across the heights, avoiding the trails and anywhere that Dopey might be. It seemed he was slipping into a new life without Beau. Even in his dreams he was alone, as though his brother had better things to do than hang around with him in the night. But then, as spring was turning to summer, he dreamt that Beau had come home. It was different from the dreams he'd had at first, when he'd seen Beau only for a moment. This dream went on for days, and Beau was back, and nothing had changed. No one even asked where he'd been. He was just *there*, as though he'd never gone away.

Danny couldn't figure out what it meant. But the dream bothered him so much that he told his mother about it, and she said it meant that Beau would never disappear from his thoughts. "All you have to do is think about him, and he's with you," she said. "He'll always be with you."

But on a day in June, Danny suddenly realized that he'd gone more than a whole hour without thinking of Beau. He found that happening more and more, and remembered the satellite dream, and now saw what it had meant all along.

There was one very sad day in that month, when a letter came for Beau. Danny saw it on the kitchen table when he came home from school. He could see right away that it had come from Cape Canaveral, because it was marked "Cape Kennedy," a name that Beau had never said aloud, a name he'd hated. He remembered Beau saying, "They never shoulda changed it."

Two hours later, the Old Man came in and found it, and he started crying.

It sat there all through dinner; then Old Man River reached out very quickly and picked up the envelope and tore it open. Inside was a very short letter. It said:

Dear Beau River,

Thank you for your letter. If you would like more information about the Gemini space program, you might start at your public library. If you're ever at the Cape, there is a public museum dedicated to the astronauts and their efforts in space. We would be delighted to offer you whatever assistance we can.

Sincerely,

Gus Grissom

Danny asked if he could keep the letter. He put it back in the envelope, and put the envelope on Beau's table, just where he thought Beau would have kept it himself. Then he moved it to the shelf above Beau's headboard, because he thought Beau would probably have moved it there so that he could read it every night before he went to sleep.

Every second day, Danny took out the letter and read it aloud.

thirty-one

On the first day of his summer vacation, Danny sat on the porch looking at the grass that had grown over the Old Man's pit. He was thinking that someone passing for the first time would never guess there had *ever* been a hole there. He started thinking, too, about how everything had changed, but nothing looked any different. The grass and the sky, the trees and the creek, they didn't care that Beau was gone. They didn't even notice.

Then he happened to look up, and saw a dog on the big bridge at the end of the Hollow.

The bridge was a long way away. To anyone else, the dog would have been a speck, smaller than a mite of dust. But Danny could tell not only that the dog was black and white but that it stood looking into the Hollow. Then it began to move, and Danny watched it trudge along, as though it was very old. It flickered behind the railings of the bridge, until the houses and the lay of the land hid it from Danny's sight.

He went back to looking at the grass, remembering how he and Beau had built snowmen right there, how they'd stretched out on their backs one summer night to watch meteors streak through the sky. He remembered how they'd made fifty cents cutting the grass before the Old Man started digging.

Again he saw the dog. It had come into the Hollow and was now plodding up the street toward the house. Its body was white, with a black patch like a saddle. Its legs were white, its head was black, and it kept its nose near the ground, sniffing along the street.

Danny watched it curiously, because he had never seen this dog before. He felt a little spark of happiness inside him and, without thinking, made a whistling sound with his lips. The dog raised its head and lifted its ears. A white tail swung up and waved at him, and the dog hurried a bit, though it seemed half lame.

There was nothing new in any of this. Every few months, perhaps four times a year, a wandering dog found its way to Hog's Hollow. Of course they all ended up near Danny River. His mother had always said that Danny was like a magnet for dogs. Once, he remembered, Beau had laughed and said, *No, Danny's a magnet for fleas. The dogs just come along.* The memory felt both happy and sad.

The dog reached the grass and nearly doubled its speed. At any time before "the accident," Danny would have leapt up to meet it. He would have run over the grass, then dropped down in a crouch, and he and the dog would have greeted each other the same way, with their little bows and wriggles. Then he would have coaxed that dog into the house—not that it would have taken much coaxing. He would have fed it cheese from the fridge, and cold milk in a bowl. He would have called for his mother and told her, "Look. It must be a stray. Can I keep it?"

But now he barely moved. And that was to turn the other way. He didn't want the dog to come right up to him; he didn't want to have to pet it and stroke it.

He heard its claws on the concrete. He heard the swish of its tail, and the whine that it made. Then he felt its nose rubbing at his arm, and he jerked that arm away as though the nose had been fiery hot instead of cool and damp.

"Go away," he said.

But the dog tried to jump up at him. It planted its forefeet in his lap and reached up for his shoulder. The claws scraped higher on his arm, and he felt the warm breaths puffing in his ear.

"Go *away!*" he said again, and shoved the dog with his elbow.

It fell away but was back in a moment. It clawed at him more frantically now. It muttered and mewled.

"Buzz off!" said Danny.

He was scared to touch the dog. He was scared of feeling happy when he shouldn't, of forgetting about Beau as the grass and the sky had done. He got up and went into the house.

He sat in the empty living room, hearing the dog claw at the door.

His mother came in with a basket of laundry. He could smell sunshine and summer on the clothes, and knew she had just taken them down from the clothesline. She looked at him and asked, "What's that noise at the door?"

"It's a dog," said Danny.

The curtains were drawn, but the windows were open, and the cloth sucked up against the frames. The door rattled, and the dog cried out.

"Were you playing with it out there?" asked Mrs. River.

"No," said Danny, as though playing with a dog was a shameful idea.

"Well, I'm sorry, but you can't keep it," she said.

"I don't *want* it," said Danny. "I wish it would go away." He raised his head and shouted at the door, "Buzz off, you stupid dog!"

Mrs. River looked at him over her basket of laundry. The clothes were puffy and white, like a ball of cotton candy. "Danny," she said, "why are you sitting in here and the dog is out there?"

Danny shrugged. He wasn't sure he really knew, and he was certain he couldn't explain it.

"Maybe you should walk it up from the Hollow," said Mrs. River. "It might go home on its own."

"I don't want to," said Danny.

The door rattled more loudly. The dog's whines became howls. Danny folded his arms and scowled at the carpet.

"Oh, Danny." Mrs. River put down her basket. She sat beside him on the long sofa. "You can't keep hoping that everything will go back to the way it was," she said. "What's done is done, and we have to go on. You wouldn't be doing anything bad to Beau if you went and had some fun." She touched his blond hair, smoothing it back from his forehead. "Isn't that what he would want? Don't you think he'd be sad to see how you are?"

He was surprised that she'd come so near to what he was thinking. He had never imagined that Beau might be sad because he was sad himself. But he wasn't sure, and he said, "It doesn't matter."

"No, Danny, it *does* matter," she said. "We've lost Beau. We've lost him forever. But I don't want to lose you, too, and I am. I'm losing the happy little boy that I knew, and it breaks my heart."

The dog was still clawing at the door, up and down the wood. "Great balls of fire, do something for him, Danny," said Mrs. River. When he didn't move, she went to the door herself. With the sound of the latch the clawing stopped, and when Mrs. River opened the door the dog was just sitting there, looking up, its head at a tilt and the tip of its tail tapping on the porch.

"My goodness," she said. "He's just a puppy, Danny."

He had to lean out from the sofa to see the door. Mrs. River was down on one knee, and the dog was nuzzling against her. It was true, he saw now; the dog had walked like an old-timer, but it was really very young.

"He's all ragged," she said. "The fur's all matted, and his ribs are sticking out. He's starved half to death, Danny. Gracious, his little paws are worn away. Danny, he's been walking for days, the poor thing."

He watched her hands rubbing the dog's back. They slid over the dark saddle and over the white, and the dog was gazing up at her, quiet and happy. The fingers circled under the neck.

"He's got no collar. No tag," she said.

"Don't let him in," said Danny as she stood up.

"I don't believe my ears," she said. "Danny, for heaven's sake, don't you care?"

"If you let him come in, he'll never go home," he said. He heard in his voice an exact echo of his mother. How many times had she said that to him?

"Danny, we have to at least take him to the pound," she said. "We can't let him keep wandering; he won't last very long. You watch him for a minute until I get my purse and keys."

"Just close the door," said Danny.

"Oh, fiddle-dee-dee, you do what I tell you," she said.

So Danny rolled off the sofa and slouched to the door. His mother came away and he took her place, blocking the entrance like a security guard. He tried not to look down, but couldn't help it, and saw the dog's huge eyes staring back.

"Don't look at me like that," said Danny. "Man, you're an ugly dog." It had huge, sticking-up ears and a short nose.

It whimpered at him. Then it held one little foot in the air, and Danny saw blood matted in the white hair around the claws.

His heart softened a bit. He felt it sag in his chest, and he blew out a long breath, the way his father would do. He crouched on the floor, in the doorway, and took the dog's paw in his hand. Gently he turned it so that he could see the pad.

It looked tender and sore, just the way his own knees had looked after Creepy Colvig had made him pick up the broken bottle. He could feel it trembling, and the dog was looking at him with eyes so big and brown that Danny had to turn away. Then the dog put down its head and licked the back of his hand, from the knuckles to the wrist.

"Quit it!" said Danny, pulling his hand away. The warm tickle of the dog's tongue had made him shiver.

The dog whined. It flopped onto its belly, then rolled upside down with its little white legs splayed out. Danny could see that all four of the pads were worn away, as though someone had taken a belt sander to them. He could see the dog's ribs, and the pink skin on its stomach, as tight as a drum.

He heard his mother coming up behind him. "Now, that's more like it," she said.

"Maybe you should put iodine on his paws," said Danny.

"Well, I don't know about that," said Mrs. River. "I don't know what's best for dogs. Pick him up and take him to the car, Danny, please."

"If he's walked so far, he can walk to the car," said Danny.

"Please?"

"Oh, okay!" said Danny. He stood up, and the dog stood, too. It leapt into his arms as soon as he reached toward it, then wriggled against him, trying to lick his face.

"Quit it!" he said again. But he couldn't stop himself from giggling.

"I don't want him in the front," said Mrs. River. "He might cause an accident. Maybe you should sit with him in the back."

But Danny said the dog would be fine on its own, and he opened the door with one hand, and the dog jumped in. It found the little hollow that had been made by Beau's weight, and it turned a quick circle and settled there, as though in a nest. It was asleep before Mrs. River got the car turned around.

Danny kept looking back at it as they drove through the Hollow, up the hill and over the big bridge. This was the first time a dog had ever ridden in the car, and he was glad that he hadn't sat there with it. He didn't want to start liking a dog that would be gone in ten minutes.

The dog stayed asleep until Mrs. River stopped the car at the pound. There were muffled barks coming from the building; when the engine shut off they could hear them. Then the dog stood up and looked out, and made the strangest, saddest sounds Danny had ever heard. It had a peculiar way of whining and grunting and howling all at once.

"It's like he's trying to talk," said Mrs. River.

"I think he knows where we are, Mom," said Danny.

"Well, he hears the dogs," she said. "He probably smells them."

"It's a sad smell, I guess," said Danny. There was a look of misery on the little dog's face. It turned away from the window and stared at him, then suddenly bounded up at the back of his seat. It clawed at the upholstery, yelping and whining. It seemed to be pleading with Danny; then it turned and pleaded to Mrs. River. It jumped up and down, scrabbling frantically at the seat.

"Oh, Danny, this is horrible," said Mrs. River. "Even I don't want to leave him here. Your father's going to have to deal with this."

She started the car again and backed it up. The dog stopped whining but didn't sit down. Its paws on the back of the seat, its eyes just peeking over the top, it looked out through the windshield.

"We'll go to the vet," said Mrs. River. "We'll get the vet to look at those paws."

thirty-two

The veterinarian was Dr. Dennison. In his waiting room, among the potted plants and the magazines, sat a frail old lady with a birdcage, and a budgie that had no tail. She looked toward the door as Mrs. River came in, and then at Danny with the black-and-white dog in his arms.

She had a pointed face, and a beak of a nose. "I hope that dog's not a bird-eater," she said, her voice a near twitter. "That's what happened to my Timothy; a bird-eater got ahold of him. You keep that dog of yours under control, young man."

"He isn't my dog," said Danny.

"He should be on a leash," she said with a sniff.

"Oh, fiddle-dee-dee, he can barely walk," said Mrs. River. "So I scarcely think he'll leap at your silly little bird."

Mrs. River and Danny sat on a black bench, below a plastic tree. The dog curled between them, resting its chin on Danny's lap until Danny nudged it away.

They could hear a cat howling in the examining room. With each howl the budgie twitched and the old lady frowned more deeply. Then out from the room came an enormous man with a tiny kitten in his hands. The man was crying.

The bird lady picked up her cage. "Hang on, Timothy," she told the budgie, and went into the room. Just moments later she came out again, not looking happy at all. Dr. Dennison stood in the doorway, telling her, "Look, I'm sorry, but there's no such thing as artificial feathers. You'll see; they'll grow back soon enough."

But the old lady didn't answer, and Dr. Dennison closed his eyes and shook his head. Then he smiled at Danny. "You can bring your dog in now, son."

"He isn't mine," said Danny.

Mrs. River had to carry the dog. She set it down on a metal-topped table, in a room that was white and hospital-smelling. Dr. Dennison patted its head. "What's your name, buddy?" he asked.

"He doesn't have a name," said Mrs. River. "He's a stray."

The vet nodded, then beamed at Danny. "He followed you home, did he, son?"

"No, he didn't," said Danny. "If he'd tried, I wouldn't have let him."

Dr. Dennison's smile faded. He was wearing a white coat, and he fiddled with the end of a stethoscope that was clipped round his neck. "Well, what seems to be wrong with our little stranger?"

"His feet are worn away," said Mrs. River.

The vet leaned forward, and the dog lifted a front paw, as though it understood what was happening. Dr. Dennison examined its paws, then felt its belly and its ribs. He listened to its heart through his stethoscope.

"Well, the pads are worn—you're right—but there's no infection," said Dr. Dennison. "He's thin as a rake, and he needs a good wash, but apart from that he's in very good shape. He's young, you know. Not more than three months old. I'd say he's spent half his life walking."

"Poor thing," said Mrs. River.

Dr. Dennison took a biscuit from a box, a brown biscuit shaped like a bone. He put it down in front of the dog, and the dog lay down to eat it. "You might try rubbing Vaseline on the pads," he said. "But what he needs most is a rest and a bit of love. Look after him, and he'll be as good as new in a week."

"What sort of a dog is he?" asked Danny.

"What sort *isn't* he?" said the veterinarian with a small laugh. "He's got a bit of everything in him, I'd say. Collie and shepherd; there's some Lab in him, too. It's like he's trying to be whatever you want him to be."

"But I don't *want* him," said Danny.

The dog lay flat, looking sadly at Danny.

"I've never met a boy who didn't want a dog," said the vet. "But you won't have any trouble finding this one a home, if that's what you want. He's a smart little guy, and he's going to be a beautiful dog."

"He's ugly," said Danny.

"Oh, you can't judge him yet. He'll grow into those ears." Dr. Dennison tickled the dog's neck. "Sometimes the ugliest puppies become the most beautiful dogs. It's the same way with people."

"I know!" said Mrs. River. "My older boy, Beau, he was born so ugly—" She stopped in midsentence, then looked down at her big Bible-shaped purse. "He had an accident," she said softly. "Just a while ago."

"I'm sorry," said Dr. Dennison. He looked from her to Danny, who had become very quiet and glum, and it seemed that he understood—just as the dog had done—everything that had happened.

"Here, son. Take him." He picked up the black-and-white dog and held it out for Danny. But Danny turned away.

"Now, it's all right to love a dog, son," said Dr. Dennison. "Doesn't mean you don't love something else." He offered the little dog again, but Danny wouldn't take it. "I think you'd find that if you loved this one, you'd get more in return than you'd ever imagine. Have you noticed that he never takes his eyes off you? He wants to be with you, son."

"All dogs want to be with Danny," said Mrs. River.

"Well, I don't want to be with *him*," said Danny. "I'll never own a dog." He turned and left the room.

He sat in the car, his feet not quite touching the floor. He sat all alone, thinking of Beau. When his mother came out, she was carrying the dog. It settled again into the shallow nest on the backseat.

thirty-three

Danny wanted nothing to do with the little black-and-white dog. But the dog wanted only to be with Danny. It followed him all through the house that day, from the kitchen to the living room, from bedroom to basement.

Danny never fed it, never touched it, never spoke a kindly word, but there it was at his heels, limping on its tender feet. Danny pitched it three times from Beau's chair and twice from Beau's bed. "You keep off there!" he shouted. "I can't wait for you to get better and leave."

When Old Man River came home, Danny was outside on the porch, and the little dog was on the other side of the door, scratching at the wood, yapping and whining in its voice that was almost like talking.

"What's that noise?" asked the Old Man, coming up the stairs. "It sounds like a bag of monkeys."

"It's a dog," said Danny. By his tone, he might have said, *It's a* rat!

Old Man River stopped on the stairs. He gave his cap a tug. "There's a dog in the house? Does your mother know?"

Danny nodded. "She brought him in."

"Ho!" laughed the Old Man. "Has hell frozen over?"

He went past Danny. The moment he opened the door the dog came out. It came squeezing through the narrowest space, while the door was still swinging. But it didn't dash for Danny. It welcomed the Old Man, bouncing up all around him, yelping with a desperate whine. Its paws could reach no higher than the Old Man's thighs, and they kept slipping off the green coveralls, so the dog stumbled and fell and bounced up again, more frantic than before.

"Down, down," said the Old Man, though his eyes were shining and his mouth was stretched in a huge smile. "He's like old Nelson. He's just like old Nelson," he said.

Well, Danny had seen the picture of old Nelson, and he didn't think *that* dog was anything like *this* dog. "He's stupid," he said. "I hate him."

"Then why's he here?" said the Old Man.

"I think Mom likes him," said Danny.

"Ho!" barked the Old Man again. "Then you don't know your mother." He bent down and patted the dog, and Danny felt a jolt in his heart, though he wasn't sure why. It was the first time a dog had ever gone to someone else instead of him, and the first time he had seen his father pet one. His father's big hands came down, and the dog jumped into them, soaring up to wriggle and lick at the Old Man's neck.

"Yuck!" said Danny.

"The spitting image!" cried the Old Man, grinning past the dog. "Why, it takes me back twenty years to do this, Danny. It takes me right back to Pearl Harbor."

Danny gaped. His father had never, ever spoken of Pearl Harbor. "Were you there, Dad? Were you really there?" he asked.

"For a while," said the Old Man. The dog was whining, and he had to raise his voice. "Not the day they attacked. I was there later."

"Wow!" Danny wasn't the least disappointed by that. "Did you see the *Arizona*, Dad? Did you see the *Missouri* and—"

"Yes, I saw it all, Danny boy," said the Old Man. "But there's nothing to tell you. I didn't do anything you'd want to hear about."

"But, Dad—"

"Why are his feet so sticky?" The Old Man—now suddenly the hero of Pearl Harbor—was holding the dog like a baby, upside down in his arms. "Danny, what's all this on his feet?"

"Vaseline," said Danny. "His feet were sorta ragged. The vet said he's been walking half his life."

The Old Man looked shocked that they'd gone to the vet. He asked how much vets cost; then he took the dog into the house, calling out, "Flo! Where are you?"

Danny stayed on the porch, but he could hear through the door as his parents argued. He heard his father asking why they were spending money on strays, and his mother saying, "It isn't a stray. Not anymore."

"What do you mean?" said the Old Man.

"I want to keep him," she said. "I want Danny to have a dog."

"But he doesn't want it," the Old Man said.

"Oh, fiddle-dee-dee. He wants it more than anything on earth," she said. "He just doesn't want to *admit* it."

thirty-four

The dog came to stay in the old gray house in the Hollow. Mrs. River fed it breakfast and dinner, and the Old Man took it out in the yard after dinner, sitting to watch it as he cleaned his teeth with a toothpick.

But still it was Danny the dog followed around, hobbling on its bruised feet. That was the only time it ever moved, when Danny went from room to room. Otherwise, for the first ten days, all it did was sleep, waking every few hours for a drink of water and a bit of food. As the days went by, the dog and the boy became closer.

There were things that Danny wouldn't allow—that he would never allow, he thought—like the dog wanting to sleep on Beau's bed, and the dog's habit of pulling Beau's things from closets and shelves.

A hundred times a day he told it, "You can't touch that,"

or "You just leave that alone." He snatched from its mouth Beau's model rockets, and Beau's books and even Beau's Pez dispenser. He had to put Beau's letter from Gus Grissom back on its shelf, after the third time he found the dog pulling at it.

There were times, too, when having the dog around nearly broke Danny's heart. He would be concentrating on something, all his mind on a task—like the balancing of the top story of a card house—and he would hear his mother talking. And for an instant, in a small and secret part of his mind, he would think that Beau was there, that she was talking to Beau. His heart would flutter, and in this tiny instant he would feel so happy, and wonder why it seemed so long since he'd last seen Beau. But then the instant would pass, and he would know it was only the dog out there, only the dog trying to worm its way in, to take the place of Beau. And in those moments, he hated the dog.

There was one time when he hated it so much that he hit it. He was lying on the floor, making a birthday card for the Old Man—it was going to be the Old Man's birthday—and the dog was lying against his feet. That was always where the dog was now—on the floor by Danny's feet, or up on the couch by Danny's feet. Old Man River had made a joke that the dog was like "a big bunny slipper, you know? Those big furry bunnies?"

His mother came in from outside and called from the kitchen, "Where are you, the two of you?" Beside him, the dog woke up, and the sounds and the feeling were like Beau was there. Danny's heart fluttered.

That instant of joy came and passed in the turning of his head. He saw the little dog, with its huge ears sticking up, and he swung his arm and slapped it.

The dog made no sound. It flinched away and closed its eyes, then blinked three times at Danny.

Danny River had never hit a dog in his life; he had never *dreamed* of hitting a dog. He saw the look of hurt and wonder in its eyes, and he threw down the pencil that he'd been using, twisted around, and hugged the dog in his arms.

Then Mrs. River came into the room and saw him. "Oh, that's nice," she said. "That's nice, Danny."

He didn't tell her what had happened, but he told the dog he was sorry. He whispered in one of its giant ears that he was sorry, and that he would never do it again.

thirty-five

On the eighth of July, in the morning, Mrs. River got out her Vaseline and examined the dog's feet. Every morning she had done that, then rubbed in the jelly. But now she didn't open the jar. She put it back on the shelf. "He's healed," she said. "He's all better."

Danny looked down at her from his breakfast chair. The dog was lying on the white tiles, with all four of its legs sticking up.

"So now what, Danny?" asked his mother.

He didn't know what she meant at first.

"You wanted to take him to the pound as soon as he was better," she said. "Should I get the car keys now?"

Danny had completely forgotten that they were keeping the dog only until it was well enough to send away. That sick, hollow feeling came into his stomach as he imagined

driving up to the pound, carrying the little black-and-white dog out of the car.

"Mom!" he said. "I don't want to take him back." He got down on the floor. "Please, I want to keep him."

He looked up, and she was smiling. "That's fine, Danny," she said. "But there's only one thing."

For an instant he was terrified that she would tell him, "The city's no place for a dog." But all she said was "I'm not keeping a dog that doesn't have a name."

"Okay. Okay," said Danny. It seemed terrible to him now that the dog was still just *the dog* or *that thing*. "I don't know what to call him," he said.

"Well, how about Rhett?" she asked. "For Rhett Butler, you know; the handsome fellow?"

"But he's ugly," said Danny. Quickly he added, "A little bit ugly." In truth, the dog didn't seem half so ugly to him anymore, but he didn't want to admit it.

"Then how about Yankee?" asked Mrs. River. "Here, I know! Yankee Dog. What about that?"

Danny shook his head. He made a face, as though he'd bitten into a lemon.

"Oh, fiddle-dee-dee. You come up with something," said Mrs. River. "Why don't you take him out and think about it?"

She left him alone with the dog—the two of them down there on the floor. Danny hadn't thought about names for dogs since Beau had his accident, and the long list that he'd kept in his head now seemed old and forgotten, like an ancient book with cobwebs all over it. He remembered Billy

Bear but didn't want that anymore. It reminded him of Billy Bear lying in the ground in the backyard, and that reminded him of Beau lying in the ground, and he hated thinking of that. He wanted a name that would make him happy, not sad, when he said it.

Then he remembered that Beau had made suggestions, and he thought it might please Beau somehow if he chose one of those. Laika; that was one. And Barker. (He remembered how he'd laughed, and wondered if that had hurt Beau's feelings.) But Barker didn't fit the little black-and-white dog. Whiner or Yelper, he thought, but those were no good.

Then he heard Beau's voice, as real as anything, just as he'd heard it in their secret fort on a day that seemed both long ago and only minutes past. *When you get a dog you should call it Rocket. That's what I'd call a dog.*

He could see Beau leaning back on the wall of the fort, chewing on a long piece of grass, his legs crossed at the knees, with one foot swinging up and down. But Danny wasn't sure if that was true or just made up. He knew only that the words were right. *Call it Rocket. That's what I'd call a dog.*

Danny looked at the black-and-white dog. In a fast whisper he said, "Rocket." The dog didn't move. "Rocket," he said again, louder. "Hey, Rocket!" But the dog just lay there, still on its back, with its huge ears spread out like wings.

It occurred to Danny that maybe his dog was deaf. So he clapped his hands loudly, and was pleased to see how it

startled to its feet. He stood up himself. "Come on, Rocket," he said. "Let's go down to the creek."

They went out through the back and down through the woods, and the little dog stayed right behind Danny, leaping over small sticks and tiny hummocks of grass, its ears flapping. They didn't go anywhere near the Colvig house, but the other way instead, down to the pools where Danny had made his dams in the days before the accident. It was the first time that he'd been back there, and he was surprised to see how summer had made the place so tangled with bushes. There were bees all around him, and sparrows in the trees, and Highland Creek was a lazy little trickle.

Danny worked his way downstream, hopping from one bank to the other every time the bushes closed in. Rocket went with him, leap for leap.

When they were under the bridge, where the creek was widest, Danny stopped. Big chestnut trees leaned over the shallow pool where he'd staged his naval battles. He could remember whole fleets of stick boats milling here, and the prickly chestnuts with all their tiny spikes had been his floating mines.

Danny sat down, and Rocket sat beside him. "I used to come here with Beau," said Danny.

Rocket tipped his head and stared at him. Those big ears turned and quivered.

"That's Killer Hill over there," he said, pointing downstream, under the bridge. "We used to go sledding there, me and Beau."

The dog whined.

"Yeah, it makes me sad," said Danny. The cars hummed by above them, rumbling on the bridge. Birds pecked and whistled in the branches of the chestnut trees. Down the creek, on the golf course, he could see men moving along, and sometimes the flash of the sun on the shaft of a golf club.

"You want to go swimming?" said Danny. He nodded toward the water.

The dog didn't move. It just sat and stared at him.

"It's not too deep. I'll show you," said Danny. He took off his shoes. Then he took off his socks and stuffed them into the shoes, and he hiked the legs of his jeans into bundles round his knees. He stood up and waded into the water, feeling the mud ooze between his toes. He walked out to the middle, with the brown creek surging past his legs. The pool was speckled by shadows—from the branches of the chestnut trees, and the streaks of the cars going by.

He turned around to call for the dog, and saw that Rocket was already swimming behind him. The dog paddled along with its ears floating, the tip of its tail poking up like a periscope. "That's good," said Danny. He walked backward across the pool, watching his dog, and he could feel in his heart that he was falling in love with Rocket.

They walked farther down the creek that day than Danny had gone in many weeks. They kept in the shallow canyon of the creek, and Danny watched for garter snakes in the tufts of yellow grass. He kept looking back at Rocket, worrying that he was going too far or too quickly. Each time, at the sight of the dog there behind him—*his* dog behind him—he felt happy and proud.

He had gone so often with Beau this way that he imagined Beau was with him. He could almost feel his brother there, as though his ghost was walking with him. He felt that Beau was happy, too.

thirty-six

When Old Man River drove down to the Hollow that evening, trailing smoke from the stacks on the big pumper truck, Danny was waiting in the garden. The boy and the dog were playing tug-of-war with a bit of rope.

As soon as the truck came to a stop, the dog dashed away to meet the Old Man. He leapt up at his front and up at his back, jumping so high that he jingled the keys on the Old Man's hip. Round he went, like a tetherball around a pole, and the Old Man didn't even push him away.

"Okay, good boy," said Old Man River.

"Hey, Dad," shouted Danny. "He's got a name now. We're gonna keep him."

"That's great," said the Old Man as he came toward Danny. The dog ran ahead of him in tight little circles.

"Yeah," said Danny. "I'm calling him Rocket."

"Oh. Rocket, huh?" said the Old Man. He nodded, then tugged his cap. "Rocket. Yup, that's nice," he said, but he sounded disappointed.

"Don't you like it, Dad?"

"Sure, it's great. Course, it doesn't have to be permanent," said the Old Man. "You don't have to stick with it, Danny, if you find something you like better."

"Like what?" asked Danny.

"Oh, I don't know," said the Old Man with a huge shrug. "Like, um—oh—maybe Nelson?"

Danny shook his head. "I like Rocket."

"Well, that's settled, then," said the Old Man. "That's the end of it, isn't it?"

But it wasn't. Not quite.

After dinner that day, Danny took Rocket out for a walk. He meant to go to Killer Hill, but Rocket led him a different way, through the maze of trails behind the creek. They went up and down, and east and west, and little Rocket went zooming all over, sniffing at bushes, at tree trunks and bottles and garbage. Danny just followed along.

They went high up the slope, and back to the creek. Rocket wagged his tail and started digging in the dried mud. He scrabbled at the riverbank, flinging the dirt behind him. Then he barked in a way that sounded like a little shout, and pulled from the dirt a pair of old gloves.

Danny knew them at once. Long ago, they had belonged to his father. Then Beau had taken them and painted them with aluminum paint. They were the gloves that Beau had worn on Halloween night, when they'd come to wash a bucket in the half-frozen creek.

Rocket dragged one of them over the ground, then looked up at Danny with a bright gleam in his eyes. He barked again before taking one glove in his mouth and shaking it hard. He shook it furiously. The glove slapped his nose, and his own ears slapped the sides of his head, and in his throat he made little growly sounds.

Watching this, Danny didn't know what he felt. It was funny to see the little dog attacking a glove. It was strange that he'd found it. But mostly it was sad to see the gloves again, to remember that night and what they had done, to remember the feud in the Hollow. That was pretty well over now, the feud. Danny figured the Colvigs had won.

He took the glove from Rocket. He held it to his nose like an oxygen mask and smelled for the scent of Beau. But it was only dirt he smelled, and worms. So he stuffed both of the gloves back in the hole that Beau had made. He thought how his fingers were doing exactly what Beau's had done. Rocket, lying down in the dirt, watched without moving.

"It's okay," said Danny. When he was sad, Rocket was sad—that was what he noticed then. They both had been so happy, and now both were so quiet. Rocket was peering up as though he felt guilty for what he had done.

"Really, it's okay," said Danny. "Don't worry. You didn't know about the gloves. You didn't know what they were."

Rocket barked. He got up when Danny did, and they

both arrived home covered in mud and thorns. They arrived to find the Old Man in the kitchen, with his big green box from the attic.

After the gloves, seeing the box now was almost too much for Danny. He felt a hotness in his eyes, an itching in his throat.

The picture of Nelson was lying on the table beside the box. The sailor's shirt, the crushed hat, and the trousers were piled on a chair, and the Old Man had the album of big, thick pages in his hands, opened across his lap.

"Ah, Danny boy," he said. "I wanted to show you a picture of Nelson. I thought maybe you might reconsider and name your dog in his honor, so I went up and got this." He touched the cracked picture, sliding it toward Danny. "But you've already seen it, haven't you?"

Danny nodded. There was never anything gained by lying to a septic man.

"It's funny, isn't it?" said the Old Man. "Here I'd thought you'd found the spitting image of old Nelson, but they could hardly be any different. They've both got four legs and a nose. They've both got a tail and—well, that's where it ends." He let out one of his little chuckles, but it didn't sound like a laugh. "I never should have looked, Danny boy."

Rocket had settled right under the Old Man's chair. Danny could hear the television in the living room, and the creaking of a chair as his mother turned in it. She would be trying to hear what they were saying, trying to ignore the television.

"There was this in the box," said the Old Man. He lifted the album from his lap and brought out from underneath it a bit of rusted metal, the name tag of Billy Bear. "This was in there with the string hanging out."

Danny touched his throat, as though he still might find the tag hanging there.

"Now, I won't ask how it got inside here," said Old Man River. "That doesn't matter now. But tell me, Danny. Did you and Beau look at everything? Did you go through all the pictures?"

"No," said Danny in a squeak that he could hardly hear himself. He shook his head.

"But did Beau figure it out?" said the Old Man. His hand was shaking, and the thick pages knocked together. "He must have, didn't he? He figured it out, why I'm a septic man today."

"No, Dad," said Danny. "He thought it had something to do with the war, that's all."

Under the chair, Rocket whined. Danny wished he could bend down and pet him. He wanted to feel the dog's fur.

"You sure about that?" The Old Man turned the pages in the book. Danny saw pictures of people and beaches, of trucks and trees, but they were all upside down to him.

"Danny, do you know what I did in the war?" the Old Man said. "I went out to Pearl Harbor in a ship. From San Francisco. I was seasick all the way. Didn't see anything except the inside of a bucket. I was so sick that they put me in the hospital when we got to Pearl, and I never went to sea again. They found me a job that kept me on shore. Danny, they sent me out to pump the septic tanks. I drove all around Hawaii, pumping tanks at Pearl Harbor, at Hilo and Wakeham Field and . . . The war killed my ambitions, Danny. When I came home I found a job doing the only thing I knew how to do. It wasn't supposed to be forever." He closed the book. "So there's your big navy hero, Danny. A seasick swab pumping septic tanks. Did Beau know about that?"

"No, Dad," said Danny. "You were always his hero."

"Come here, son."

Old Man River put the album on top of the jacket and trousers. He put Billy Bear's name tag on top of that. Then he brought Danny to his side and hugged him in his arms. Rocket looked up from the floor.

"Was Beau proud of me, Danny?" asked the Old Man.

"Sure he was, Dad," said Danny.

Rocket came to his feet. He stood on his hind legs, trying to force himself between Danny and the Old Man. He was whining.

"What about Gus Grissom? Did he ever say he wanted to go and live with Gus Grissom instead of me?"

"Why would he say that?" asked Danny. "Heck, Dad, why would he want to do something like that?"

Mrs. River called out from the other room. "Charlie? What's going on out there?"

"Oh, we're just shooting the breeze," said the Old Man.

"Why's the dog crying?"

"He wants up, I guess," said the Old Man. "He feels left

out." So he patted his knee, and Rocket jumped onto his lap.

Danny rubbed the dog's head, and the Old Man rubbed its back, and Rocket seemed happy then, practically grinning at the two of them.

"Rocket's a fine name," said the Old Man. "He's your dog, sure enough. He was born to be with you, I think."

Old Man River put his album and jacket and the rest of his things back into the green box. He gave Danny the name tag. "I don't know what you want to do with this," he said.

Danny could still see, and feel, the letters stamped into the metal. "I think I'll bury it with Billy Bear," he said. "Maybe Billy Bear wants it more than me."

The Old Man said that would be fine, and he gave Danny a hug. "Maybe Rocket will help you," he said.

"Yeah, he's a real digger dog," said Danny.

Rocket sprang down to the floor, sliding on the tiles in a hurry to keep up with Danny. The Old Man chuckled. "He loves you already, Danny," he said. Then he added, in a moment of unthinking, "Before you know it, the two of you will be closer than brothers."

Danny stopped in the kitchen doorway. He turned around slowly.

"I shouldn't have said that. I'm sorry." The Old Man was slumped in his chair. "I don't mean you'll forget about Beau. I don't want you to even try to do that. You'll always have Beau with you now, you understand?"

Danny nodded, and went out. Rocket came with him,

down the three steps and over the grass toward the place where Billy Bear was buried. The crosses that Danny had made still stood above the little graves, but Billy Bear's had fallen sideways.

Danny buried the name tag, and that was that. It felt to him that something had been finished, like a short chapter in a long story. It was as though Billy Bear had come awake for a while, just to teach him things about his father and his brother, and now was sleeping again, in the shade of the old gray house.

thirty-seven

Saturday was the day that Danny dusted Beau's models and books, the day that always made him feel sad. As he went from one thing to another, dusting and remembering, Rocket watched him from Beau's bed.

He didn't mind anymore that Rocket slept there. He would have liked it better if the dog had slept with him, but Rocket was happiest wedged between the pillows on Beau's bed—most often sprawled on his back, his eyes moving with the slow turns of the airplanes hanging above him.

This was the first time that Rocket was in the room as Danny dusted. The dog had always been locked out, left to scratch and cry at the door. Danny had wanted to be alone with his memories, but now he shared them with the dog.

"This was the first model he made," said Danny, dusting

a Spitfire with a crooked wing. "See, he put the decals on upside down."

The dog whined.

"Yeah, he felt pretty stupid about it," said Danny. He moved on to the next model, a Mustang that seemed to be soaring from a little pedestal shaped like a claw. "I gave him this one. He always said it was his favorite, but I don't know—he never hung it up with the others. See, those are his best ones hanging up there."

Rocket barked.

"Sure, he liked it *okay*," said Danny.

He worked his way along the shelf, and the dust that he swept away glowed in the morning sun. It swirled in silvery shafts and made the room churchlike and peaceful. The balsa-wood biplanes turned ever so slowly, and their strings sparkled in the sun. A feeling came over Danny that Beau was there with him, in the silence and the glow that floated around him.

He studied each thing he picked up, then returned it precisely and gently to its place. When he moved from the shelves to the desk, Rocket jumped down to the floor and stood by the closet. Tail wagging, nose thrust out, he barked at the door.

"I don't like looking in there," said Danny. But the dog kept barking, so he turned the handle and opened the door, and Rocket tried to press through it, howling into the darkness.

Danny looked into the closet. On the floor was the big

Rocket Base USA, and that was what the dog was barking at. For once, those huge ears lay flat on the dog's head, and Rocket bounced back with each bark, hopping clear off the floor on stiff little legs.

"Hey, stop it," said Danny. "Quit it, Rocket." He was bothered by the barking, a crazy sort of noise. He grabbed the dog, and it shook in his hands like a little motor. "Look, Rocket," he said. "Look, it's just a toy."

But it was a big, hulking sort of toy, and Danny could see why it might frighten a dog. In the closet's gloom, its missile launchers pointed in four directions. The black helicopter sat on its pad, and the white astronauts lay toppled on the platform at the top of the turret, as though they'd fallen asleep at their places.

"You better go on now, Rocket," said Danny. He pushed the dog away. "Go on," he said, and Rocket went running from the room. Danny heard him scamper down the hall, then turned to tidy up the Rocket Base.

He didn't touch the dials and gauges and levers. They were still set just where Beau had fixed them on the day of his accident. But Danny stood the astronauts on their feet again, and made sure that the missiles were fitted into the launchers. He regretted not doing it before, when he'd first carried the base in from the garden. He wished he'd restored it to the way it had been. But even now, as he worked, the memories that came out of the Rocket Base weren't happy at all. They weren't even happily sad, like the ones glued up in the plastic Mustang. He could still see himself running after the little rockets, and Beau crouched over to aim them and fire them. It occurred to him now that Beau might still be alive if they hadn't played with the Base that day. And the worst thing of all . . . it had been Danny's idea to use it.

He was crying as he put the missiles into place, in the launchers on the top and the silos on the sides. There once had been eight, but now there were only six. One was hidden in the grass where Beau was buried, but Danny had no idea where the other was. He imagined that the yellow machine had churned it into the ground, and that it wouldn't show up again for thirty years, like the bones of Billy Bear.

The feeling of the church in the room, and of Beau being with him, was gone. He felt small and pitiful as he sat hunched on the floor, the tears trickling over his lips. He sniffled and swallowed as he worked on the toy.

He hadn't quite finished when Mrs. River called him away. "Danny!" she shouted. "Come and see your dog!"

He went running to the kitchen. She pointed out the window and showed him where Rocket was standing at the edge of the street.

"He came to me in a terrible state," said Mrs. River. "He was hopping around, barking like mad, all anxious to get out." She rapped on the window and shouted at the dog. But Rocket didn't move. "Now he won't come back, Danny. If I go out there, he moves away."

"I guess he's mad at me," said Danny.

"Why?" she asked.

"Just 'cause I put him out of the room," said Danny. "I was cleaning Beau's things, and telling him about Beau, and he started barking at the Rocket Base. He was bugging me, Mom."

"The Rocket Base?" she said. "Danny, why were you showing a dog things like that?"

"I was . . ." He couldn't explain, so he only shrugged.

"I think it's time we got rid of some of those things," she said. "It's not fair to you to have them around."

"No, Mom," he said. "I don't want anything changed. I want it all to stay the same."

"But it's *not* the same," said Mrs. River. "It's never going to be like it was. I want you to see what's wrong with Rocket. I'll talk to your father about this."

She went down to the basement and packed away her novel. She hadn't opened her notebook since the day of Beau's accident, and knew she never would again. The novel seemed stupid to her now, her dreams of money as ridiculous as the Old Man's fallout shelter.

As Mrs. River put away her notebooks and her pencils, Danny went out to help Rocket. He found it was just as she had told him: when he got close to the dog, the dog moved away. Rocket watched him come closer, then twirled around and ran a little farther down the street. In darts and dashes, the dog led the boy toward the head of the Hollow.

"Quit it," said Danny. "You can't go that way, Rocket. It's where Creepy Colvig lives."

Rocket was barking at him, ready to dash again toward the end of the Hollow. So Danny walked away and didn't go back, though the dog kept barking. Finally, Rocket came after him, his tail limp and drooping, his eyes blinking sadly.

"We can go for a walk, but not that way," said Danny. They went over the big bridge instead, up to the heights and toward the school. Rocket sniffed at every fence and every tree, then trotted on and sniffed again. Soon the dog was leading the boy, and Danny began to wonder if Rocket wasn't following the route that had brought him to the Hollow in the first place. He wondered if Rocket was going home.

All the dogs that Danny knew came running to see him. They brought their balls and sticks and laid them at his feet. But Danny didn't want Rocket to feel jealous, so he only petted the dogs briefly before moving along. Where he had always left a trail of happy, panting dogs behind him, he now left them staring glumly up the street.

They ended up at the school. Rocket sniffed across the parking lot, between the portable classrooms, up and down the steps to the school's front doors. On the gravelly baseball diamond, they found a group of boys that Beau had known. They'd once been friends of Beau and Danny both, until the accident had changed all that. Rocket went wagging up among them, and they stooped to pet him but didn't have much to say. "Howzitgoing, Danny?" they asked, and "How's Old Man River?" Then they picked up their bicycles, slid their gloves over the handlebars, and went flying away down the street in a V like a flock of geese.

Danny watched until he couldn't see them anymore. Rocket was lying at his side, watching too, and he whimpered as they vanished round the distant bend. "It's all changing," said Danny. "Everything's changing."

That reminded him of his mother and what she had said about Beau's things. A sudden fear came over him that she was packing them away right then, maybe stacking them by the road for the garbageman. The thought became so real in his mind that he took Rocket through the woods, though it would bring them near the Colvig house. He ran faster than he'd ever run in his life, his head down, as though it might hide him from Dopey. Rocket bounded like a rabbit, those big ears flapping.

They crossed the wooden bridge and came out on the grass. Danny paused there a moment, all sweaty and breathless, and pointed out the Colvig house for Rocket. "You stay away from there," he said. "Don't ever go near it, okay?"

Rocket tipped his head. To Danny, he looked worried.

"Now let's go," said Danny.

There was nothing piled outside the old gray house, and that was a huge relief to Danny. The pumper truck was in the driveway, and the Old Man was waiting in the kitchen. He greeted Danny with a big, fake smile, as wooden as a ventriloquist's dummy's.

"Hey, there you are!" he said, sounding too loud and too jolly. "I've been thinking, Danny. That dog of yours hasn't seen the A&W yet, has he?"

"No," said Danny. The smile had made him wary. Whenever his father was too jolly, something bad was soon to happen.

Old Man River clapped his hands. "Hey, how about we take him there now?"

"Sure. Okay," said Danny. He thought it would

disappoint his father if he said no. But he could guess what was coming. All the way to the Dub, the Old Man would talk about things that didn't matter. He'd pretend that his hamburger was the best thing he'd ever tasted. Then he'd wipe his mouth with his hand and say, "Oh, by the way . . ." And out would come the bad news.

Danny followed the Old Man out to the driveway. He climbed into the truck and saw with surprise that Rocket hadn't followed him. The dog had come only as far as the porch, to the top of the stairs. The Old Man, one hand held up to the steering wheel, whistled and said, "Come on, boy."

Rocket sat down.

"Danny, you call him," said the Old Man, his smile gone already.

Danny did, but nothing changed. Rocket sat stubbornly at the top of the steps.

The Old Man wrenched his cap. "For crying out loud! Go and get him, Danny."

Danny went back and crouched by the dog. He smoothed its ears. "What's the matter, Rocket?" he said.

The dog looked back at him through a shaggy fringe of fur. Its eyes seemed huge, circles of black in circles of golden brown. Rocket whimpered softly. The Old Man shouted for Danny to hurry. "I don't want to stand here all day," he said.

Danny ran his hand over the dog's head, down along its back. "You like riding in the car okay," he said. "Why don't you want to go in the truck?"

The boy looked eye to eye with his dog. He looked *through* those eyes and into its soul, and saw a thing that he could hardly believe. Suddenly his hand was shaking with the possibility of it. "Holy man," he said.

His voice fell to a whisper. He put his face inches from Rocket's and stared more deeply into those huge rounds of eyes. He saw spots of light and curved reflections, and all the sky and the grass and himself shrunken to fit in the circle of black, and he was almost certain then that he was right. "Beau? Is that you?"

Rocket's tail slashed madly. His ears perked up, and he shot out his tongue to lick Danny's nose.

"Beau," whispered Danny again. The tail lashed harder; the tongue slobbered and licked. "You're back. Oh, Beau, you're back," said Danny. He cuddled the dog, and he wept.

thirty-eight

The Old Man was getting quickly impatient. "I'm not that dog's chauffeur," he called from the truck. "Pick him up, Danny."

Danny kept petting the dog, rubbing his hand along the bump of its spine. "I knew you'd come back. I dreamt it," he whispered. "I saw you come back in the dream."

"Danny!" shouted the Old Man.

"I'm sorry I didn't know right away. I'm sorry, Beau," said Danny. "I didn't mean it when I said I hated you. I didn't know it was you."

The dog rolled onto its side. It arranged its legs to bare its belly for rubbing. Its eyes were more shiny than ever, glistening like pools of fresh rain.

Old Man River came along the path, his boots slapping round his ankles. He tugged his cap; he twisted it to the right. Then he stood above Danny. "That dog's not sick, is it?"

Danny shook his head.

"Then what's the matter—" The Old Man suddenly stopped talking. He bent down and looked at Danny. His voice went soft. "Have you been crying?" he said.

Danny rubbed his face into the dog's fur, hoping to dry the tears that had come to his cheeks. He was bursting with the news that Beau was back. But he thought his father would only laugh if he told him.

"You'll spoil that dog rotten like this," said the Old Man. "If he won't do what he's told, you make him do it." He reached down to pick up the dog, but Danny pushed his hands away.

"No, Dad. Let's take Mom's car," said Danny. "He'll go in the Pontiac no sweat. He just doesn't want to ride in the—"

It was on his lips to say *the poop-mobile*. But instead he said, "The pumper truck. He doesn't want to be in the pumper truck."

The Old Man turned his cap nearly sideways. "Oh, for crying out loud."

"Just try it, Dad," said Danny. "Please?"

"It's crazy," said the Old Man. "If you give him his way, he'll be running the roost."

"Please?" said Danny again. "Just this one time?"

"Oh!" sighed the Old Man. "I'll get the keys."

"We'll wait in the car," cried Danny.

The boy and the dog got up nearly together. They ran to the car, and the dog bounced at the door as Danny, laughing, opened it. Old Man River scratched his head through his cap. "Danny, I swear you're half dog," he said.

All three rode in the front seat. Danny gave Rocket the window, because that had been Beau's place whenever the Old Man was driving. Rocket put his head out into the rush of hot air, his ears flapping.

The trip went nearly exactly as Danny had thought. They rode in silence to the A&W. The lady came out in her brown-and-orange uniform and took their order. Danny said, "Rocket would like a root beer."

The Old Man was reaching for his wallet. "Well, Rocket isn't *getting* a root beer. He wouldn't like it."

"Oh, I think he would," said Danny.

The lady smiled at him. Ladies always smiled at Danny River. She told him he had a cute dog, then asked its name.

"Rocket," said Danny.

"Is he fast as a rocket?" she asked.

"No, he just likes them," said Danny, grinning at his dog.

The lady brought their meal on a tray that she hooked on the Old Man's half-open window. Neither Danny nor his father said anything about the park with its waterfall and rocks to sit on. Danny knew they wouldn't go back there, that they'd never go back. It would be too sad to see the one empty rock where Beau had always sat.

Danny unwrapped a burger for Rocket, then held out his foaming mug of root beer. Rocket sniffed at it before putting his nose through the froth to guzzle from the mug. Danny laughed. "I bet he's been wanting that," he said, grinning at his dad.

"I've never seen a dog that liked root beer," said Old Man River.

Danny used his paper napkin to wipe the dog's small shag of a beard. "Remember how much Beau liked root beer?" he asked.

"By the gallon," said the Old Man.

"You think Rocket likes it just as much?"

The Old Man had a hamburger in his hands. Now he put it down and licked ketchup from his fingers. "You think about Beau a lot, don't you, Danny?" he said.

"I sure do, Dad."

"Well, so do I," said the Old Man. "I think about him day and night. I think about him so much that I sometimes wish I could *stop*. Do you know what I mean?"

"Yeah," said Danny, looking at the dog, not the Old Man. He had moved as close to Rocket as he could, and he put an arm around the dog. "It means you're going to throw his stuff away."

"Oh, geez, Danny." The Old Man leaned across the seat, and scraps of white onion and green lettuce fell from the front of his shirt. "You amaze me sometimes, you know that? We talked about it, your mother and me, but we're not throwing anything out. We don't want to wipe your brother out of your life, Danny. We just think it would be better if some of the toys were up in the attic. We don't think you should be surrounded by everything that was Beau's."

"Yeah, okay," said Danny.

The Old Man laughed. "I could have saved myself some money here. I thought you'd be upset."

"But I get to say what stays in the room," said Danny. "Like the letter from Gus Grissom, that's important."

"Agreed," said the Old Man.

"And the fighter planes. They're important too."

"All right."

"And the bed," said Danny. "That's the most important thing. He needs the bed, 'cause that's where he sleeps."

The Old Man sighed and tugged his cap, "Now that's the thing, you see. Beau's gone, Danny. He doesn't need a bed."

"Sure he does, Dad." Danny tightened his arm around Rocket and leaned his head on the dog's ribs. He could feel the bones moving as Rocket breathed beside him.

"Oh, you mean *Rocket* sleeps there," said the Old Man.

"Yes," said Danny. "And you know something, Dad?" Danny couldn't stop himself now. "Beau's inside him, Dad. Beau's come back."

The Old Man looked as white as the little bits of onion.

"It's true," said Danny. "Look." He put his mouth to the dog's ear and said, "Beau," and the dog twitched and barked, and Danny grinned. "You see? It's him. He *knows* it's him."

"Oh, Danny." The Old Man's face was suddenly full of wrinkles. "You say Beau, but he hears *boo*. It's just a sound. It means nothing to him."

"He walked all his life to get to Hog's Hollow. He wore his feet away to get there. And he knows stuff, Dad." Danny was smiling. He was full of his feeling of joy, of the magic of it all. "You said he was born to be with me. You said he belongs here, Dad. You even said that dogs are children."

"I never said that," said the Old Man.

"You did! At the park. You said dogs are children."

Old Man River looked up at the roof of the car, then closed his eyes. "Oh, Danny, I meant that dogs *act* like children, that they play like children do."

"Why did he come straight to our house?" asked Danny.

"He had to end up somewhere, didn't he?" said the Old Man. "It's not like he's the first dog to ever want to be with you."

Danny had both his arms around the dog. "I didn't think you'd believe me right away," he said. "But you'll see, Dad. Just talk to him, and you'll see."

"Aw, this is nuts," said the Old Man. He shook his head and sat up straight. He lifted the tray from the window, then opened his door and set the tray on the ground.

"Try it, Dad," said Danny.

"No." The Old Man closed his door. He started the car and backed it out of its place. "That's a dog, Danny. It's only a dog."

thirty-nine

As the summer went by, Danny became certain that Beau was in his dog. He wondered only how it worked: was Beau really back in the shape of a dog, or was Rocket a real dog with the soul of a boy living inside him?

It was a wonderful thing to know, and Danny only wished that his parents could see it, too. They wouldn't be so sad if they knew that Beau was back. But they wouldn't talk about it, and wouldn't even *think* about it. Ever since the day he had brought it up with his father—who had told Mrs. River, bringing her to tears—it was a thing that was not to be mentioned.

Danny told Josephine. But for once it wasn't good enough to tell his secrets to a dog. He decided to tell Steve Britain, the boy whose father wet his bed, who had known Beau nearly as well as anybody had.

It was a sudden decision. He met Steve by chance at Camp Wigwam one day, when he went to play in the big teepees that sat empty through the weekends. From the edge of the woods he heard the screaming whine of a tiny engine. The sound made Rocket prick up his ears and hurry along.

Steve Britain was standing in the middle of the field, turning in place, flying his yellow Skyraider round and round on its wires. By his feet was the red jug for gasoline, and the little toolbox for his wrench and screwdriver. The plane did a loop, then flipped on its back and started circling the other way. Rocket was barking as he ran toward Steve.

Beau had spent hours flying the Skyraider with Steve, and Danny had spent hours watching them, hoping for a turn but never getting one. The sound and the smell made him remember how he'd gone dashing back and forth with the gasoline and the tools, trying to make himself useful enough that he would finally get a turn.

As Rocket ran toward him now, Steve Britain shouted, "Get that dog away!"

"It's okay," called Danny. "He knows what he's doing."

"If he gets hit, it's not my fault."

Rocket chased the plane. He ran just behind it, leaping and spinning, falling and starting again. He yapped and barked.

"Hey, quit it!" shouted Steve.

Rocket took one more turn round the circle, then veered into the middle. He sat there beside Steve, his head swiveling as he watched the plane, his tongue hanging out, his eyes like black jewels.

Danny went right up to the circle, and the yellow plane came whizzing toward him and went zooming away with the sound always changing. To Danny, it sounded like an angry mechanical cat howling: *Meeeeeowww! Meeeeeowww!* Steve was leaning back as he stepped in his steady circling. Each time he turned, the sunlight flashed on his glasses, reminding Danny of a lighthouse.

"Oh, it's you," said Steve. "Howzitgoing, Danny?"

"Okay," said Danny. They had to shout back and forth.

"Is this your dog?"

"Yeah," said Danny.

"It's some crazy dog."

Steve Britain made his airplane loop and whirl. He flew it upside down and right way up, close to the ground and straight over his head. Then the engine sputtered twice and conked out, and Steve brought the Skyraider down. It hopped along the ground like a big yellow bug.

The moment it stopped, Rocket jumped up at Steve, crying out in his talking voice of whines and yaps.

"What's he doing?" said Steve.

"He's saying hello," said Danny.

"Okay, hello. Now get him down," said Steve. He pushed the dog aside.

Rocket whirled away and ran toward the Skyraider. Steve Britain shouted at Danny to stop him. "If he wrecks it, I'll kill him," he said. But the dog only sat beside the plane.

"See? He knows," said Danny. "If he had fingers, he'd refuel it for you."

"Sure, Danny." Steve picked up his jug and his tool kit

and walked to the plane. He filled the tiny tank through an even tinier funnel. "I was thinking about Beau," he said. "Just before you came. I guess you miss him, huh?"

Danny nodded.

"Me too. I sure did today. It's hard to fly this thing alone." He put down his jug and shook the plane, flinging droplets of fuel. They sprayed across his glasses, like melting rainbows. "I heard you got a dog. He's not as ugly as I thought he'd be."

"Look in his eyes," said Danny.

"Why?"

"Just look."

Steve held his hand toward the dog. There was gasoline on his skin, already dried to a whitish powder, and Rocket's eyes blinked at the smell, but he didn't pull away. Steve smoothed the dog's fur on its nose and forehead. "Yeah?" he said. "So what?"

Danny was disappointed. "Look hard," he said. "You can sorta see through them. You can see inside him."

"Aw, get lost," said Steve. But he leaned closer. He poked his glasses into place. "There's speckles," he said. "Is that what you mean?"

"No," said Danny. The sun was behind Steve, making his face a black shadow. "I saw Beau in there."

"Man, you're nuts." Steve took his hand from Rocket's head as though the dog was hot as fire.

"He knew you, didn't he? Soon as he saw you," said Danny. "He knows all sorts of stuff like that, 'cause Beau's inside him."

"Like *My Mother the Car?*"

"Well, sorta. But better than that," said Danny. He hated that show, with the stupid car driving around, talking like the guy's mother.

"*My Brother the Dog.*" Steve laughed. "Did you tell Old Man River?"

"Yeah, but he didn't believe me," said Danny.

"No wonder. Man, people are going to think you're just crazy, Danny."

"Call him Beau, then," said Danny. "Look in his eyes and call him Beau."

"Forget it," said Steve. "You're getting creepy, Danny." He flicked the propeller on the front of the plane till the engine started, and its growls and coughs became a scream that he had to shout against. "Hold it down! Like this!" He had the plane's flat body pinched in his fingers. "Let it go when I tell you, okay?"

"Let Rocket do it," said Danny.

"Aw, get lost," yelled Steve. "Just get lost, Polluto!"

He took a nail and a paper clip out of his pocket, jammed the nail into the grass, and clipped the plane to it. Then he snatched up his tools and gasoline and dashed down the wires to his handle as the little airplane tugged at its mooring. It broke loose when Steve jerked on the line, then skittered across the grass and lifted into the air. It zoomed around in its circle. Danny ducked as it passed over him. He felt the slip of its wind in his hair, and smelled the gas and the fumes.

Danny ran from the circle with Rocket behind him.

Then he turned back and shouted, "Screw you, Britain!" and Steve laughed, the sunlight shining on his glasses. The Skyraider was howling again: *Meeeeeowww! Meeeeeowww!*

Danny went around the Hollow and over the big bridge. He felt sorry for Rocket, plodding beside him with his tail between his legs. "Never mind," he said. "It doesn't matter what anyone says. I know it's you in there, Beau."

forty

Danny lived with his secret, hoping his mother and father would see for themselves what was so obvious to him. Rocket's favorite toy was a worn old tennis ball that had belonged to Beau. He'd pulled it from the bushes by the backyard. His favorite spot in the living room was on the floor where Beau had always sat to watch TV. He slept in Beau's bed, which Danny had fought hard to keep, and he played in Highland Creek, and he loved the Old Man and Flo.

In the evenings, Danny and Rocket lay on their beds, and Danny told the dog stories. He would start, "Remember this?" and go on about something, and Rocket would lie there and listen, and sometimes he would chatter away in the funny voice that was almost like talking. There were times when Danny slipped up and called the dog Beau, and then Rocket barked back at him.

Twice he slipped up when his parents were there, once with his mother and once with his father. The Old Man just corrected him. "Rocket, you mean," he said. But his mother got angry. "You're not still full of that nonsense, are you?" she said. "You do *know* he's only a dog, don't you?"

She was standing in the bedroom doorway. She'd been listening and watching without him knowing. Now she came right into the room, right between the beds. "Tell me you know that," she said.

The room was half empty. Most of Beau's things had been put away in the attic, and the walls where his posters of spacecraft had been were huge and barren. The only thing on the long shelf above the bed was the letter from Gus Grissom.

"Danny, I'm waiting," said Mrs. River.

"I know he's a dog," said Danny.

"And that's all that he is?" Her hands were on her hips. "Say that he's a dog and no more."

He couldn't admit it, not there with Rocket beside him. He wouldn't betray his brother. So Mrs. River snapped her fingers and told Rocket, "Down!" She pointed at the floor.

The dog burst out in his whines and yaps and groans. It seemed to Danny that he was right on the verge of actually talking, and he thought how great it would be if Rocket could look up at her and say in Beau's voice, *Mom, it's okay; it's me.* But Rocket only got down from the bed, slinking from it like any old dog, his eyes squinty and scared, his tail a sad, sagging thing.

"Out!" said Mrs. River, raising her arm to point at the door.

"Please don't send him out," said Danny.

"Then you tell me that he's only a dog," said Mrs. River. "Say he's only a dog."

Rocket was looking up at Danny, and Danny could see that he wanted him to say it, that he wanted him to do anything so that he wouldn't have to sleep outside the room. So Danny crossed his fingers under the bedclothes. "He's a dog, okay?" he said.

"Yes. Okay," said Mrs. River. "But if I hear you call him Beau again, he's gone, Danny. And I don't mean just gone from this room. He's *gone*; you understand?"

forty-one

In August the days were long and hot. They passed one after the other, all the same, with an endless blue sky and a huge, white sun. In Hog's Hollow, the leaves of the big cotton-woods turned crisp and yellow, and Highland Creek shriv-eled to a thin worm of water. Its banks were hard and cracked, like the skin of a sunburned old Earth.

On the sixteenth, when the day was at its hottest, Old Man River came home from pumping septic tanks. He took off his coveralls and put on a clean shirt. He put on trousers that were pressed and spotless. Mrs. River chose a tie for him to wear, but he only stuffed it in his pocket.

"I wouldn't feel right," he said.

She had chosen a black dress for herself, and a little black hat. But her shoes were red, and her purse was red, and she'd painted her mouth with shiny red lipstick. To Danny she looked pretty.

"Now, we won't be gone long," she told him. "You won't even have time to get into trouble."

She bent down to kiss him, but he moved his head away. He was watching TV, and Rocket was sleeping on the floor by his feet. The Old Man was in the bathroom.

"I want to go with you," he said.

"Oh, we're not going anywhere you'd like to go," she said.

He hated it when she acted as though he was stupid. He knew very well where his parents were going, and why, and it made him angry that they would think he'd forgotten, as though he was only a dumb kid with no memory.

"This is something your father and I have to do," she said. "It isn't for fun."

"I know it's Beau's birthday," he told her. "You don't have to keep it a secret that you're going to see where he's buried."

"Oh, gosh, Danny," she said. "It's not a secret, exactly. We didn't want to remind you, that's all."

"You don't want me to go there," he said. "That's why you didn't tell me."

Rocket had come awake, and now he sat up, calling out in a whine. Danny knew that he'd heard his old name, and hoped Mrs. River would notice. But she didn't glance at the dog.

"It's too hot out there," she said. "Why don't you just stay inside where it's cooler?"

"I want to go," he said. "Beau was my brother, you know."

"Yes, Danny, I know that."

"You still think it's all my fault, what happened," he said.

"Danny! We've never said such a thing," she told him.

"But that's what you think," he said.

He heard the whoosh of the toilet flushing. The pump came on, dragging water from the well. He told his mother, "I bet you'd take Beau if it was me that was buried."

Her red lips opened. There was a smear of lipstick on her teeth. "What a terrible thing to say," she said. "Danny, that's horrible."

The Old Man was coming into the room, tugging at his belt. "What's horrible?" he asked.

"Danny knows where we're going, and he wants to come with us," said Mrs. River. "He says if it was him who was—" She shook her head. "I can't even say it."

"We didn't ask you to go because we didn't think you'd want to," said the Old Man. "You didn't go on Sunday, or the Sunday before."

"But today's different," said Danny. He hadn't seen any point in going to the cemetery now that Beau was back. Now, though, he wanted Rocket to see it. Or he wanted his parents to see Rocket seeing it; he wasn't really sure.

"Then go and change into clean clothes. And have a wash," said Mrs. River. "You're absolutely filthy, playing in the creek all day."

He hadn't been playing—not exactly. He had gone downstream through the golf course, looking for bottles.

He'd taken them to Mr. Kantor's and bought a present while Rocket sat waiting outside. It was in his pocket now. He'd only been waiting for the proper time; they'd always given out birthday presents after dinner.

He brought it along in the Pontiac.

The sun was enormous, the heat staggering. Danny cried out when his bare legs—below his shorts—touched the heated vinyl in the car. The Old Man gasped when he got in, and Mrs. River said, "Mercy! It's like an oven."

"It'll be better when we're moving," said Old Man River. But the air that gusted through the car as they headed up the hill only grew hotter. Mrs. River had to keep her hand clamped on her head so that her little black hat wouldn't go sailing through the window. The only one who seemed comfortable was Rocket, with his head poking out in the draft, his tongue flapping like a pink ribbon.

The cemetery seemed twice as hot as the Hollow. There were no trees for shade, and the endless rows of white crosses and stones glared like shining glass. Only one other person moved in the place—an old woman in a black gown and a black shawl, holding up to the sun a black umbrella. She looked scary to Danny, as though the white ghosts of night were black in the daytime.

Where Beau was buried the ground rose in a small hill, and climbing toward it made Danny remember the day of the funeral, and the smell of flowers, and the taste of tears on his lips. He stopped halfway up, wishing he hadn't come back this day, watching his father and mother hold each other as they reached the top together. The Old Man had his cap in his hand, slapping it against his leg. His keys jingled softly.

Rocket didn't follow Danny. He stayed beside the car, in the shade of the big tail fins.

Danny went slowly to the top of the hill. His mother was standing there in the terrible heat, and the Old Man was sweeping pigeon droppings from the gravestone. All around, the grass was yellow and dying. The lady with the black umbrella was wandering from grave to grave.

Danny sat down. He watched the lady in black, and the birds that flew in tidy flocks, and the car that came crawling along the road with four people inside, so old that they looked like four mummies out for a Sunday drive.

He felt sad, but this time not for Beau. He wished that his mother and father knew that Beau was back, that he was just down the hill, living in the little dog that sat shaded by the car. He hated that his mother was crying, and he could feel the misery that came from them both, a thick fog of sorrow and despair. Then he felt Rocket licking his hand. He turned and saw the dog's limp tail and drooping ears, and it looked as though Rocket had been soaked in the Old Man's sorrow.

The dog whined at Danny, then pressed up against Mrs. River and whined at her, and then at the Old Man. The voice that Old Man River had said was like a bag of monkeys cried out so loudly that the car stopped and the mummies looked up the hill.

"My, he sounds miserable," said Mrs. River. "Danny, take him away."

"It must be the heat," said the Old Man.

"No," said Danny. "He's telling you not to be sad."

"Please," said Mrs. River. "Don't start that non-sense now."

"But listen to him," said Danny. "He's trying so hard. He's telling you—"

"One more word, Danny, and that's it."

"Okay," he said. "Okay, I'm going."

He sat in the car, though the heat was sickening. He felt like a cookie baking in an oven, as though he might melt across the seat before he turned all hard and crisp. But he kept the door open, because Rocket was there beside him.

Up on the hill, his parents were kneeling. Danny saw his mother open her purse and take out a small box wrapped in shiny paper, tied with a sparkling ribbon. She gave it to the Old Man, and he held it for a moment before he put it down. Then he thrust his hands into the earth and dug as fast as he had the day he'd started his pit. He tore away the sod, then buried the box.

Rocket was crying his wails and whines. So Danny took out his present, a key ring shaped like an airplane, and he held it out for Rocket to see.

The dog stopped whining. He put a paw into Danny's hand, as though to touch the airplane. Then he sat up and licked Danny's face.

Danny clipped the airplane to Rocket's collar. It was a cheap little airplane. Within a day it would fall from its clip and never be seen again. But right then Danny thought it was the greatest thing in the world.

"Happy birthday, Beau," he said.

forty-two

The third Saturday in August was a perfect day. At Cape Canaveral, a great rocket stood ready for the launch of Gemini V. In Hog's Hollow, the day began shadowed and cool, and in the old gray house Mrs. River made pancakes. She made little ones for Danny, the size of silver dollars, and for the Old Man she made them huge and thick, topped with a square of butter as big as a matchbox, all drowned in maple syrup.

Old Man River set up his TV tray in front of the sofa, beside Danny in the armchair. Rocket was on the floor, but—to Danny's disappointment—he was sleeping. Danny had hoped his parents would see the dog sitting all day by the TV as intently as Beau would have done. He poked the dog with his foot, but Rocket only yawned and rolled over.

It was nine in the morning, an hour before the launch.

The Old Man hadn't shaved or combed his hair, and he looked like a hobo to Danny. When Mrs. River brought him his plate of pancakes he said, "Ahhh!"—like a miser seeing gold. He chopped out a wedge with his fork. "This reminds me," he said. "I have to pump the tank at the pancake house."

"Today?" said Mrs. River. She always waited while he tasted his pancakes.

"No, no. Sometime," he said. "It must be filling up." He smeared his wedge in the butter and the syrup, ate it, and smiled. "Delicious. No one makes pancakes like your mother, Danny."

Rocket slept through the pancakes, through the walk of the astronauts from building to gantry. The sun was flashing on the astronauts' suits.

"There's Gordon Cooper," said the Old Man. "That's him waving now."

Gordo, thought Danny. That's what Beau would have called him. It's Gordo! he would have said. Now Rocket lay in his place, flat out on the carpet like any dog.

Mrs. River made a second pot of coffee. Danny heard the bubble of the percolator, then the hiss of water boiling out onto the burner. The astronauts were sealed in their capsule; everything was ready. A small clock in the corner of the screen was counting backward to liftoff.

"Flo! Aren't you going to watch?" said the Old Man.

"I'm watching," she answered, through the door and through the wall.

Danny sensed she was thinking of Beau. He thought the

Old Man was thinking of him, too, but not in the same way. His mother didn't *want* to think about him, but his father did.

In their capsule, the astronauts were talking by radio to Mission Control. A voice answered them. "You're looking A-OK. You're go for launch."

Then Rocket woke up. He stretched his four legs, then yawned and stretched his tongue, which coiled from his mouth like a blow-out party favor.

"That was Gus Grissom giving the go-ahead," said a newsman on TV. "Grissom's the capcom today."

Rocket was watching now—or it seemed that way to Danny. It seemed the voice of Gus Grissom had brought him from his dream, and now he was staring at the TV. Danny said casually, "Rocket's watching TV."

"Well, it's right there in front of him," said the Old Man.

The clock on the screen flashed to 1:00:01, to 1:00:00. Gus Grissom spoke again. "Launch minus one hour. All systems go."

Rocket barked. He stood up.

"Look at that. He's getting excited now," said Danny.

"He wants out, I guess," said the Old Man. "Has he done his business yet, Danny?"

"He sure has," said Danny. "That's funny, he's excited now."

Mrs. River came in with the coffeepot. "Yes, why don't you take him out, Danny?" she said. "You can go up to Kantor's and get some milk. I've just finished the bottle."

"We'll miss the launch," he said.

"Oh, fiddle-dee-dee. It's an hour away, and you'll be back in ten minutes."

"But—"

"Charlie, tell him," she said.

"Do as you're told," said the Old Man.

So Danny went out, and Rocket went with him. For the first time, Danny took the dog on his bicycle, perched in front of him on the long banana seat. As he rode up through the Hollow, leaning into the curves of the road, it didn't surprise him that Rocket seemed to know how to balance, or that the dog kept trying to put his front paws on the handlebars.

"Bet you thought you'd never ride a bike again," said Danny.

He kept to the grass of the boulevards, where the air was cooler, and to the shady side of the busy street. Even on Sunday, the cars were rushing by, and the streamers on his handlebars fluttered and waved.

Mr. Kantor had his door propped open with a chunk of cement. He was pleased to see Danny, and didn't mind Rocket coming inside. "I don't like many dogs, but this one I like," he said. He patted Rocket with his long fingers, and Rocket licked his arm, dabbing at the blue numbers tattooed on the man's skin.

"Does he remind you of Beau?" asked Danny.

Mr. Kantor laughed. "A dog remind me of your brother? This would please you?"

Danny took the milk from the big cooler. He was careful to crack open the door and snatch it out, but Mr. Kantor still called to him: "Are you buying milk or cooling the city, Danny? My electricity bills are not high enough already?"

Danny slipped the plastic bag loaded with the bottle of milk over the handlebars of his bicycle. He lifted Rocket to the seat again, and set off the way he'd come. But Rocket barked and whined and put his paws on the handlebars, as though to steer the bike. "You want to go the other way? Gee, I don't know."

The dog whined.

"Well, okay," said Danny.

He knew why Rocket wanted this. It meant they had to pass Camp Wigwam and take the trails to the Hollow. It didn't matter to him if Dopey might be waiting. He didn't want to be late for the launch.

At the top of the hill, where the trail began, Danny stopped the bike. It was the first time he'd be taking those trails since Beau's accident, and he wasn't sure he wanted to do it. He saw Rocket looking so happy and eager, rocked the bike and counted down. "Three, two, one, blastoff!" he shouted. He pushed forward. "Hang on!" he told Rocket.

It was like his ride in the shopping cart, but the bike was even faster and wilder. At some of the corners it leaned far enough to touch a pedal on the ground. It clattered and bounced and flew down the hill, and the bottle of milk clanged against the front fork.

Just before the bridge, Danny touched the brakes. The bike slid sideways, straightened, then shot up the hill and took to the air. It landed perfectly, and they coasted out toward the bottom.

Suddenly Rocket turned his head and snarled at the bushes. And Danny saw Dopey Colvig sitting on a stone beside the creek.

Rocket leapt from the bike. Danny shouted as he tried to grab him. The bike slewed from the path, crashing through bushes. It jarred to a stop, and Danny tumbled off. The bottle of milk—still in the bag—smashed as it hit the ground. The bag bulged, then leaked white trickles onto the ground.

Danny could hear Rocket barking. He heard Dopey, too, hollering those wordless hoots and grunts. Then Rocket growled, and the hoots became howls. Danny struggled to his feet. He found Dopey lying in the creek, and Rocket on top of him, biting his chin and his neck.

Dopey tried to push the dog away. Rocket's teeth locked on his wrist instead.

"Stop it!" cried Danny. "Holy man, let him go."

But Rocket snarled and bit, and Dopey thrashed his arm around, and it looked like two animals in a deathly fight. Then Dopey Colvig swung his arm, and the dog went flying.

"Beau!" shouted Danny.

Rocket stopped fighting. But he didn't stop growling. He stood with his fur prickled up, his nose squashed into wrinkles, his teeth in horrible rows.

Dopey scuttled backward, rolled himself up, and went running along the dried-up creek.

"Oh, man! Oh, man!" said Danny River. "He's going to bring Creepy now."

He hauled the bike from the bushes. The broken bottle

still swung in its bag, dripping milk onto leaves and grass. "Come on," he said.

The front wheel had twisted. It rubbed on the fork, squeaking with each revolution. Danny dropped the bike in his driveway, took the bag of glass and milk from the handlebars, and ran with Rocket into the house.

His mother called from the living room. "My, that was fast." She came into the kitchen and found him standing there with the dripping bag. "What happened?" she asked.

"It broke," said Danny. "We were coming down the hill, and it broke."

"Were you hurt?" she asked.

He shook his head. "No, Mom."

"Well, you look all shaken up," said Mrs. River. "Danny, it's only milk. No use crying over spilt milk."

Danny watched the liftoff of Gemini V. Rocket sat on the floor and watched it, too. They saw the clock count down to zero. They heard Gus Grissom say, "Ignition." Then great blasts of smoke and fire spewed from the base of the rocket. The clamps that held it down fell away. The huge, towering thing started up into the air, so slowly and wonderfully.

The dog sat and stared. But Danny kept looking toward the windows. He kept expecting a knock on the door.

It didn't come till that evening. And then it wasn't Creepy Colvig at the door.

forty-three

Old Man River answered the knock. He opened the door to see two policemen standing on the porch. One was tall and one was short.

"Charlie River?" said the tall one.

"Yes," said the Old Man.

"You've got a dog here, Mr. River?"

"We do," he said.

The tall policeman was holding a sheet of paper. "We have an order here to remove your dog, Mr. River."

"What do you mean?" he said.

"We're here to take your dog," said the tall policeman. "It has to be destroyed."

"The hell you say."

"Your dog attacked a child, sir," said the other policeman.

The Old Man turned his head. He shouted, "Danny boy!"

forty-four

Danny River sat on a kitchen chair. He sat in tears on the chair as the policemen and his parents stood around him. Rocket had already been taken away and was barking faintly from the police car.

"Danny, what's your side of this?" said the Old Man. "Did Rocket bite the Colvig boy? I want the truth now, son."

Danny nodded. "But it wasn't his fault," he said.

Mrs. River was standing behind him, with her hands on his shoulders. "That Colvig boy makes Danny's life a misery," she said. "He hit him once with a realtor's sign. Did Mr. Colvig tell you that?"

"What about this morning?" asked the short policeman. "Did the boy do anything to you?"

"He scared us," said Danny.

"How?"

"He was sitting by the creek, and we didn't see him at first. Then Rocket got frightened." Danny looked from one face to another. "It wasn't his fault. You can't take him away. He was just getting back."

"Getting back for what?" asked the tall policeman. "Has the boy hurt your dog?"

"Well, kinda," said Danny. He could see that he had nothing to lose. If he didn't speak now, Rocket would be taken away forever. He blurted out, before anyone could stop him, "He's not just a dog, he's my brother."

"Danny!" cried the Old Man. His mother gasped.

From there it only got worse. Danny tried to explain how Dopey had pushed Beau into the pit, and when he pointed to the window the policemen gaped at the flat, green lawn outside. His mother looked embarrassed, and his father looked angry, and they stopped him from talking. They sent him out of the room; they sent him right out of the house.

"Go and keep Rocket company," said his mother.

So Danny went out in the August heat. The police car was parked in front of the house, and three people from the Hollow were standing beside it, staring at the lights and the decals as though the car was a UFO. Mrs. Elliot was among them. "What's going on, Danny?" she asked.

"They're taking Rocket away," he said. " 'Cause Rocket bit Dopey."

"Poor thing," said Mrs. Elliot. "He certainly doesn't look like a vicious dog."

Rocket had found some shade on the floor of the car. But the sound of Danny's voice brought him bounding to the seat, and he pressed his paws to the window. Danny touched the glass. Rocket cried to Danny with all his strange sounds.

"Heavens, he's talking to you," said Mrs. Elliot.

"Please go away," said Danny. "Please leave us alone."

They all went away. They touched Danny's shoulders and his blond hair, and then wandered slowly. Danny pushed his fingers through the tiny crack that had been left at the top of the window, and Rocket stood up to lick them.

"You gotta bust out," said Danny. "You can't let them take you where they're going."

Rocket looked back at him through the window. Their faces were inches apart, and one was as sad as the other.

forty-five

It sounded to Mrs. Elliot, who had stopped down the street, as though the boy and the dog were talking. It was the most heartbreaking thing she had ever seen, poor Danny River touching one side of the glass and the dog the other, and both of them talking and crying.

She wanted to hurry back and comfort the boy. But instead she went home and hugged her little Josephine to her breast.

Her curtains were half closed to keep out the sun, and she stood behind them, staring out.

She watched as the policemen came out from the Rivers' house. She saw little Flo River drag her boy back from the car. She saw tall Charlie River stooped like an old geezer. Then the car drove off, and she saw Danny break free from his mother to go running behind it. "Stop!" he shouted. "Please stop."

The car went faster and drew away from him. It passed her house, and she saw the dog in the back window, standing up on the seat to look out the back window. And she saw little Danny stop running. She heard him scream, "The fort! The fort!"—which made no sense to her. Then she saw him all alone in the street, and she thought that if a boy could ever really fall to pieces, it would happen to Danny right then.

forty-six

At five o'clock that day, barely an hour after they'd left, the policemen returned to the old gray house in the Hollow. They walked toward it from their car, with the tall one carrying a closed-in cage.

It was Old Man River who opened the door to them for a second time. Danny was lying on the living room sofa. Mrs. River kept dabbing the boy's arms and forehead with a cloth she dipped in cool water.

The tall policeman spoke up. "Is the dog here, Mr. River?" he said.

The Old Man got angry. "You know damned well he isn't here. For crying out loud, what have you done with him?"

"We lost him," said the policeman. "He got away from us."

On the living room sofa Danny opened his eyes. A smile came to his pale face, and he whispered, "He busted out. I knew he would."

"Mr. River," said the short policeman, "this whole business upsets us as much as it upsets you."

"I doubt that very much," said Old Man River.

"But if the dog comes back, you'll have to call us," the policeman said with a little redness in his face. "You'll be breaking the law if you don't."

"Goddamn your laws," said the Old Man.

Danny came into the hall, wet from his mother's dabbings. The policeman said, "Look, son, I'm—" but Old Man River cut him off.

"Don't call him 'son,' you hear?"

The policeman turned even redder. "Dogs always come home," he said. "We'll be watching the street."

The policemen left with the empty cage. Old Man River closed the door.

"Danny," he said, "don't get your hopes up. If Rocket comes home, we have to turn him in. We don't have a choice."

"He won't come back," said Danny. "I told him not to."

"Well, if worst comes to worst, you can get another dog." The Old Man was kneeling on the floor now. "You can have one right away."

"I don't want another dog," said Danny. "I want Rocket."

"I know you do," said the Old Man. "But listen to me."

Danny put his hands over his ears. The Old Man pulled

them down and said, "You can't escape it, Danny. The only one who can save Rocket is Mr. Colvig, and he's not going to do that, is he?"

"No," said Danny.

"No," repeated the Old Man. "We heard things today—your mother and me—that we didn't know. Like a bucket of sewage in the Colvigs' car. Like—"

"He bit Dopey 'cause Dopey pushed him in the pit," said Danny. "He bit Dopey 'cause he's Beau."

Old Man River held Danny by the shoulders and shook him. "You get that nonsense out of your head. Do you hear me?" He kept shaking until he shook tears from Danny's eyes. Then he stopped and stood up. "This isn't the time to talk," he said.

"Why don't you believe me, Dad?" asked Danny.

"Because it's just plain crazy," said the Old Man.

"But he promised he'd always hang around with me. No matter what," said Danny. "Then I dreamed he was back, and you said he was with me, and Mom said the dog came to find me, and . . ." He was rubbing his arms. The marks of the Old Man's fingers were on his skin. "And Mr. Kantor said people can be animals."

Danny saw his father swallow, the lump in his throat going up and down.

"Oh, Danny," said the Old Man. "Mr. Kantor spent four years living in a place like a kennel—like a zoo—but worse. He was beaten and starved and worked nearly to death. What he meant was that people can be terrible."

"I don't think so," said Danny. "And anyway, Creepy isn't the only one who can save Rocket. So can I. 'Cause I know where to find him."

"Where?" asked the Old Man.

"I can't tell you," said Danny. "I promised not to tell anyone. Not even under torture."

forty-seven

Danny went up to the fort he'd built with Beau. He crossed Highland Creek behind the house and followed its banks downstream. At the end of the Hollow, where the woods weren't as thick, he saw the police car driving slowly along the street.

He crouched behind a bush and waited until the car was far up the Hollow. Then he ran along the trails and down the ravine.

When he came to the fort, he found it in ruins. The walls were torn apart, the plywood panels broken. The things that he and Beau had stashed in there—the old bottles and moldy magazines—were scattered all around.

There was no sign of Rocket.

Danny sat and waited. All evening he waited as a thunderstorm came rumbling toward him. The sky grew dark. The wind picked up, and the trees creaked and swayed, their leaves seeming to whisper. Then rain came down, and thunder rolled across the sky, and flashes of lightning glared through the Hollow.

Danny made a tent from the plywood pieces and sat inside it, waiting. Leaves came swirling down. Little runs of water trickled through the tent, and he heard Highland Creek growing fast and strong. He began to think of the stories he'd heard, about kids who'd been murdered in the ravine. He could hear the traffic on the big bridge, and soon the headlights of the cars and trucks were making eerie shadows all around him.

His little tent was very dark and lonely. He huddled in the middle of it, staring out at every sound. It seemed to him that hours passed, that the whole night slid by. It was long enough, at any rate, that he began to doubt that Rocket was coming. And if Rocket didn't come . . . Well, he didn't want to think about what that might mean.

He sang songs to himself, about marching ants and bottles of beer. He sang until he heard something moving outside, something breathing in the bushes.

Then out of the woods came Rocket. He came slowly, and then in a dash with his tail wagging and his tongue hanging out, chattering away like a bag of monkeys. He threw himself at Danny.

"I knew you'd come," said Danny.

He held on to Rocket more tightly than he'd ever held on to anything. The thunder rumbled, and the traffic roared along the bridge, and Danny held on to the dog. "We can't go home," he said. "We can't ever go home." He could feel Rocket's heart beating quickly.

"I don't know what to do," he said.

Danny wondered if Mr. Kantor might help him, or if the vet might help. But he could picture either of them picking up the phone and calling his mother or the Old Man. He could almost hear Mr. Kantor's voice. *You let a boy and a dog run loose? What were you thinking?*

There was no one in the Hollow, or anywhere in the city, who could help him. The thought made Danny very lonely. In the whole world there was no one.

"Hey!" said Danny suddenly.

Rocket barked.

"What about Gus Grissom?" Danny cried out the name, and Rocket cried back with a whimper. "Do you think Gus Grissom might help if we went down to the Cape? Do you? Do you think he would?"

It seemed Rocket had gone crazy. He was jumping up and down, barking and barking.

"Okay. Okay," said Danny. "It's a long way, but I think we can get there."

The boy and the dog sat together until the thunderstorm had passed. Then, with the lightning flashing far away, they headed down the ravine, through the golf course in the darkness.

For half a mile, Danny walked in the creek. He made sure that Rocket did the same thing, and they splashed together through the water. "It'll hide our tracks," he said. He had seen cowboys do this on *The Rifleman* and *The Big Valley*.

Danny hadn't known there was an end to Highland Creek before he found it that night. His friendly little stream ran into a dirty river that flowed through concrete banks, carrying fleets of paper cups, and plastic bags like jellyfish, and sticks and cans and bottles. He followed it with Rocket, toward the lights of the city, great towers of light, and the roar of traffic and people.

He didn't know how to get to the Cape. "But one thing's for sure," he told Rocket. "It's too far to walk."

Where the river flowed into a huge cave of a culvert, the boy and the dog came up to the city. They looked as though they'd come from the jungles, or as though Danny really was the hillbilly of Hog's Hollow, stumbling for the first time into civilization. He was pushed and shoved along the street, and Rocket went in turns and darts with his tail between his legs.

Danny tried to stop people and ask them for money. He was certain the Old Man would be furious if he knew, but there was no choice, he told Rocket. "We gotta get to the Cape."

He touched people's arms, and pulled at their sleeves, and if they didn't stop he followed them along. But no one would listen when he tried to explain. He never got farther than "Excuse me, mister."

The crowd pushed him along to a wide, busy street. A big green sign hanging above it said SOUTHBOUND, with an arrow pointing at a lane. Danny followed it along, with Rocket at his heels. He followed it for seven blocks, then up a spiral and onto a highway. Huge trucks hurtled by in blasts of hot air, spraying water from the rain-wetted road. Like a flat, broad river, the highway seemed to flow and ripple in the moving of the headlights, the red flashings of the brakes.

Danny had gone a mile, maybe two, when he found a transport truck parked on the shoulder, its rows of taillights flashing. The driver was walking beside it, stopping at each wheel. He gave each one a kick, then a whack with a tire iron, before bending down to tighten the wheel nuts.

Danny stopped him near the back of the trailer. "Excuse me," he said.

The driver was wearing a very battered cowboy hat. He had a cowboy's mustache that hung down on each side of his mouth.

"Does this road go all the way to Florida?" asked Danny.

"It better," said the driver. "I'm lost if it doesn't."

"Is that where you're going?" said Danny.

"Yeah. Through Choo-choo Town and the Big M." He bashed at the tire with his iron. "I'll be in the Bikini State day after tomorrow."

"Can I go with you?" said Danny.

The driver touched his mustache. "You running away from home?"

"Sorta," said Danny. "I have to get to the Cape. I gotta save my dog."

"Well, I can't help you there. I'm sorry," said the driver. "There's a rule: no passengers."

He tightened the bolts on the wheel, shoving down on the iron until they groaned. "You shouldn't even be on the highway," he said. "If Smokey comes along, you'll be spending the night in the bear cave."

"Couldn't you take us just a little way?" asked Danny.

"And hang my ass in a sling?" The driver shook his head. "Just turn around and go home, kid. That's what you'll end up doing anyway."

On the other side of the trailer, cars and trucks were racing by. The noise was loud and endless. Danny followed the driver to the very last wheel, right at the end of the trailer. He tried to follow him back along the side that faced the highway, where the traffic went by only inches away. But the driver chased him off. "Go on. Get going," he said.

Danny plodded again along the shoulder, down the length of the trailer. As he reached the cab he heard the big diesel engine running. Smoke rose from the two chrome stacks, where flat lids chattered on their tops. The door was high above Danny. But a small window was set into its bottom corner, and he tried to peer through it, into a cab that seemed as big as a house. "Gee, I wish we could ride in there," said Danny to Rocket. "Bet it's got a bed and everything."

Rocket put his forefeet on the step.

"Hey, the guy said no," said Danny.

But Rocket kept pawing at the step. Danny watched for a moment, then suddenly bent down and looked between the wheels. The driver was halfway along the trailer. "Okay, come on," said Danny.

He held Rocket in one arm, climbed up the step, and

opened the door. The light came on in the cab, and he was sure that the driver would notice. There were two gearshift levers, and more gauges and dials than he'd ever seen in one place. Behind the seats was a bed that stretched across the cab, with a tartan-colored sleeping bag spread untidily across it. Danny climbed in and closed the door.

A wall divided the cab from the bed. It was solid behind the seats, and open in the middle, and Danny pulled Rocket into the corner behind the driver's seat. He bundled him among a pile of clothes. There were socks that reeked, and trousers stained with oil. But Danny didn't mind. He only worried that his own wetness—and the dog's—was soaking the driver's clothes.

"Don't make a sound, now," he said.

There was a clatter outside as the driver stowed his tire iron. Then the door opened and he came in behind the wheel. He tossed his wet cowboy hat onto the passenger's seat, shook his arms, and groaned. "Getting too old for this," he said.

With a hiss of air from the brakes and a roar from the engine, the big truck started moving. It went forward in surges as the driver worked his gears, then swayed as he pulled into the traffic. He changed to a higher gear, to another, and Danny felt the truck moving faster.

He heard a click, and the crackle of a radio, and the driver said, "Beantown Bob, you gone?"

A little voice answered. "Ten-four, Buffalo. I'm backing off the hammer here."

"Roger," said the driver. "We got twelves."

There was a crackling burst that Danny couldn't understand.

"Yeah, ten-twelve," said the driver. "Look for me in your mirror."

Danny liked the sound of the driver's voice and was sorry when he stopped talking. Other people babbled away, but he couldn't understand many of the words. It was like listening to people gargle. He leaned back and held Rocket as the truck went thundering south.

He found that he could lean against the back wall of the bed and see out through the small window at the bottom of the passenger's door. There was nothing to look at but blackness, until the truck pulled into the passing lane and the taillights of cars went flashing past the window. The hum of the tires and the shaking of the truck put Danny to sleep very quickly.

forty-eight

Danny woke to find that the truck had stopped without him knowing. It was sitting in a fuzzy glow of red and yellow lights, with the traffic sounds all muffled and quiet. His neck felt stiff, and one of his legs was pricking with pins and needles.

Rocket was already awake, lying flat on the bed, looking out through the gap between the seats. It seemed to Danny that the driver was gone, but still he looked out very slowly and carefully. He noticed first that the cowboy hat was missing, then saw the empty seat behind the wheel.

They were parked at a diner, and another truck was parked nearby. In the big windows of the diner, two men were sitting at a booth with orange-colored benches. One was wearing a cowboy hat, and when he lifted his head Danny saw the big mustache.

He smelled french fries and coffee and bacon. He could nearly taste the odors, so strong that they made his stomach roll from hunger. Rocket's nose was twitching like a living thing, and Danny felt more sorry for the dog than he did for himself. "I bet you can smell the gravy on the fries," he said. "The mustard and the pickles. Even the little seeds in the hamburger buns." He wished he could know what it was like to smell rocks and plastic, to pick out any smell among a hundred others. It would be like seeing, he thought, but through his nose instead of his eyes, seeing pictures of smells.

He leaned back in the corner of the bed, and when he heard footsteps in the gravel he pulled Rocket next to him. The driver came in, tossed his hat to the seat, and got the truck rolling. He pulled back on the highway. Into the radio he said, "Hey, Beantown, don't go feeding bears now."

The big truck was soon barreling along again, taking Danny River south toward the Cape. He started thinking about what he would say to Gus Grissom when he got there. He imagined himself and Mr. Grissom in a long conversation, and he imagined the astronaut saying, *Of course I believe you. Who wouldn't believe you, Danny?*

The driver's voice shocked him. "Hey, kid. You hungry back there?"

Danny didn't move. The driver said, "You copy, kid?" He laughed. "Come on, I know you're there. You've been snoring so loud you blew my doors off."

Danny asked in a small voice, "Are you angry?"

"Just come on up, kid."

The driver flicked his cowboy hat to the floor, and

Danny moved into the seat. Rocket sat on his lap. From the floor, the driver brought up a paper bag. There was a sandwich inside it, and the boy and the dog ate it together as they rode south toward Florida.

The other truck was right in front of them, lit like a ghost by the headlamps. In the corners it faded away, then reappeared in a bright glare as the road straightened. Danny saw little flares of fire and sparks flaming from the smokestacks.

"That's Beantown Bob," said the driver. "He keeps his toenails on the front bumper."

"Where are we?" asked Danny.

"Three hundred miles from where you started. You've been catching Z's five hours now."

The voice of Beantown Bob came over the radio. "Your ten-twelves still asleep?"

The driver smiled at Danny. He took up the microphone and answered. "No, I got the rug rat here beside me now."

Danny felt foolish. He remembered the driver talking about twelves when he first came into the truck. "You knew all along I was here," he said.

"For sure," said the driver. "I figured what the hell, you were safer with me than hiking down the super slab."

In the darkness he looked like a nice man, with that big mustache and shaggy eyebrows. He said, "Nice dog. What's his name?"

"Rocket," said Danny.

"Heading for the Cape with a dog called Rocket." The driver laughed. "You nuts about space, or something?"

"Not really," said Danny. "I called him Rocket on account of my brother."

"Yeah? So where's your brother now?"

Danny wasn't sure what to say. The cab was shaking and bouncing a bit. Yellow lines flashed toward them on the blackness of the road.

"Hey, never mind. The less I know, the better." The driver held out his left. "I'm Cody. But they call me Buffalo."

Danny shook hands.

"And you are . . . ?" asked Cody.

Danny said the first name that came to his mind. "I'm Beau," he said.

They drove through the night and through the dawn, hurtling past gray fields and sleeping towns. Danny held his dog and looked out through the windshield, or down to the small window by his feet, where a gravelly shoulder was whizzing by in an endless blur. He thought it was hotter here at sunrise than Hog's Hollow had ever been at noon.

Beantown Bob kept them going at full speed. "Doing it to it," said Cody. There was a pounding roar from the diesel, and they drove in the smoke and the dust of Beantown Bob.

To Danny, Cody was like a king of the highway, sitting there in his big throne. The cab made the Old Man's pumper truck look puny. Cody could look out for miles, and seemed to own all he could see. He drove with his arm propped on the open window, and the air whistled round his mirrors. He had traveled like that so long and so far that his left arm was tanned to the same brown as the leather on his seats, while his right arm was pale. His mustache trembled in the shaking of the cab.

For miles they didn't talk. Then Cody said, "So what's the hurry to get to the Cape?"

"I have to see someone there," said Danny.

"Who?"

"Gus Grissom."

Cody looked across the cab. "Mercy sakes! The astronaut?"

Danny nodded.

"That's bodacious. You know that guy?"

"No," said Danny. Rocket had been dozing on his lap but now was awake. "But he said he'd help my brother, so that's why I'm going to see him."

The road turned and climbed uphill. Cody bore down on the bumper of Beantown Bob. The hill steepened, and both trucks slowed to a crawl. Cody crept up the hill so close to Beantown's rig that the back of the trailer was all that Danny could see in the windshield.

"He's got a fat load," said Cody, shifting down through the gears, his hand moving from one lever to the other while his left foot pumped at the clutch. He grinned at Danny. "Hey, if I took you to the Cape, would I meet that Grissom guy?"

"I don't know," said Danny. "Maybe."

"Well, let's give it a shot." Cody pulled on a chain hanging from the roof, and the air horn blasted. He looked in his mirror, swung the truck to the left, and went thundering ahead of Beantown Bob. With his left arm hooked through the steering wheel, he worked a gearshift lever in each hand, throwing them forward and back. The diesel thundered away.

"I won't ask your business there," he said. "It's none of mine, and that's for sure. Maybe you want to log some more Z's, Beau."

But Danny was too happy to sleep. He sat there in the wind and the heat, watching the highway roll past the truck, and the fields and the towns going by.

"We'll be in Florida by midnight," said Cody. "At the Cape before dawn."

Danny River hugged his dog. "It's going to be okay," he whispered. "Everything's working out."

The sun crossed above them, then shone in through Danny's window, and the big truck kept heading south. They passed a field of cotton, a row of billboards. Then Cody looked in his mirror and said, "He's on our tail."

"Beantown Bob?" asked Danny.

"No, it's Porky Bear."

Danny heard the siren, coming up behind them. He leaned forward and looked in his side mirror, and saw lights flashing blue and red on a car that was closing quickly.

Cody slowed the truck. "Guess we'll be getting a Christmas card from Smokey," he said.

He pulled onto the shoulder with the air brakes hissing. The police car stopped behind him.

"Sit tight now, Beau," said Cody, opening his door. "It's just a local yokel. He won't even look in the cab."

But he did. The sheriff gave Cody a ticket, then climbed

onto the step and looked right in at Danny and Rocket. He asked Cody, "Who's the kid?"

"Beats me," said Cody. "Never seen him till this morning, Sheriff." He winked secretly at Danny. "I picked him up just a few miles back. Maybe an hour ago. Says he's going to the next town."

"Is that true, boy?" asked the sheriff. He had a brown uniform with a silver star on the front.

Danny nodded. What he thought was a very clever lie came right to his lips. "Yes, sir, I live there," he said.

The sheriff had a sunburned face and white eyebrows. The sun glinted on his badge. "So, what's the name of this next town, boy?"

Of course Danny didn't know; he didn't have a clue. So he sat there with Rocket on his lap, and he scratched his head and told the sheriff, "Gee, I forget."

"You forget where you live, boy?" The sheriff laughed. "Maybe I should drive you down there. See if it makes you recollect something."

"I'm going right by," said Cody.

"Then I'll save you a stop, won't I?" said the sheriff. "Come on down from there, boy."

Danny's legs were trembling as he got down from the high cab. He held Rocket in his arms and followed the sheriff toward the car.

"Hey, Beau, I'm sorry," said Cody. "All the good numbers to you now, you hear? Looks like you'll need them."

The sheriff opened the back door of his car. "In you go. *Beau.*"

forty-nine

The sheriff kept Danny all day in the cell. The lady came down twice to see him, the first time with her donut and Orange Crush, and then with a basket full of fried chicken and crisp potato skins, a small bottle of milk, and a Donald Duck comic book.

She unlocked the door herself that second time. She came in but didn't sit down; she was in a hurry, she said. "I have to be getting along home?" she told him, turning it into a question. "I 'spect you'll be the spending the night, but you won't be alone. The sheriff? He'll be sleeping upstairs? On a cot in his office, you understand?"

"When can I go?" asked Danny.

"Just as soon as you tell us where your mom and dad are at," she said. "We'll get you back to them right away. You and your little dog."

It seemed to Danny that she didn't really want to leave him, but she did. She closed the door gently so that it wouldn't rattle and bang, then looked in at him through the bars. Danny had already opened the basket and was eating the chicken.

"You're such a nice-looking boy," she said. "I wish I knew how such a nice-looking boy could get himself into such a terrible fix."

She clucked her tongue and shook her head and left him. Danny heard her walk up the stairs and talk with the sheriff for a moment. Then the door opened and closed, and she was gone.

Danny ate his chicken, sharing fifty-fifty with Rocket. He read his comic book aloud, and the dog lay down as though to see the pictures. Danny read every story, and he read the ads in the back, because Beau had always wanted to own the X-ray glasses and the Sea Monkeys. "You think they're real?" Danny asked Rocket now. "There's no little monkeys that swim around in the sea, is there?"

He was reading the stories for the second time when the sheriff came down.

"I can hear you up there, talking away to your dog," said the sheriff. "Holy moley, boy, just tell me where you've come from."

Danny didn't even look up from the comic. He paused for a moment in his reading, but that was all.

"Why, you're stubborn as a mule," said the sheriff.

The office door opened and someone came in, calling, "Hello?"

"I'm down here," said the sheriff. "Beating my brains out."

Into the corridor between the cells came a woman who was small and pretty, with a canvas bag hanging from her shoulder. She was a grown-up, but not very old. To Danny, she didn't look much different than the big kids at his high school. She had hair that was long and silky, like the mane of a unicorn.

"Not much going on today, Alice," said the sheriff. "Car went in the ditch up by the Corners. Oh, and Neddy Brown fell off of his tractor again. That's about it."

"Who's this?" asked the lady, looking in at Danny.

"Boy from up north," said the sheriff. "Runaway. Hauled him out of a rig on the highway, him and his dog."

The lady smiled at Danny. "Hi," she said.

"Hi," said Danny grudgingly.

"I'm Alice," she said. "I work for the paper."

"She's a reporter," said the sheriff, "so mind what you say." He laughed. "Not that you'll say much." He told Alice, "Kid only talks to his damned dog."

"Well, it's a nice dog," she said. "I'd talk to it, too. Looks like a terrier, is he?"

Danny shrugged. He imagined what she would say if he told her, *No, he's my brother.*

"What's his name?"

"Rocket," said Danny, caught off guard.

The sheriff grunted, and the lady came closer to the bars. "Hi, Rocket," she said.

Rocket jumped off the bed and went to see her. He

licked the hand that she held down, then whined and moaned in his bag-of-monkeys voice.

"What a little sweetheart," said Alice. "He's more than a terrier. I don't know what all's in him."

"He's part person," said Danny with a sly look.

The dog kept talking. "You know, I believe it," said Alice.

Danny River liked her then. He asked the sheriff if he could talk with her alone, and after the sheriff left he said, "Do you want to hear a story? But you can't tell anyone else, okay? You gotta promise not to tell the sheriff. He'll send me home."

"I promise," she said. "Cross my heart, and hope to die if I tell him."

He started with the day when Old Man River had thrust his shovel into the garden, and went on from there. He even told her his real name. "It's not really Beau," he said. "That's my brother. I'm Danny River." Alice put her canvas bag on the floor and sat on the bed, and it was the first time that anyone had listened to the whole thing. She listened without interrupting, without telling him that he was crazy; she listened as though she *believed* him.

He told her nearly everything, leaving out just one thing—exactly where he'd come from. He told her about Hog's Hollow, but not what city it was in. He told her about stowing away in a truck owned by Buffalo Cody, but not where it happened. She kept nodding and smiling, and that made him tell more.

When he finished, she just looked at him, and then at

Rocket. She shook her head—not to show she doubted him, but from the shame that he was sitting in a jail cell.

"Why didn't you tell your parents this?" asked Alice.

"I tried to," said Danny. "But they wouldn't listen. They said they would even take Rocket away."

"Really?" she asked. "They must be horrible."

"Oh, no," said Danny. "They're not horrible at all. You'd like them a lot. It's just . . . They don't understand stuff sometimes."

"Will you tell me again?" said Alice. "The whole thing?"

"Sure," said Danny.

"Can I record it? Do you mind?" She picked up her bag and took out a tape recorder. Danny marveled at the machine. He had never seen a tape recorder up close, and never one as small as this, no bigger than a good-sized box of chocolates. "I don't want to forget it," she said.

"Can I hear my voice?" asked Danny.

"Sure," said Alice. "As soon as you finish."

"I mean first," said Danny.

"Well, it might be better if we wait," she said.

So Danny began all over, and he thought he was as clever as Jim Hawkins in *Treasure Island*—that book his father had never finished—who had told the whole story, "keeping nothing back but the bearings of the island."

But in the end, Alice tricked him.

fifty

The first reporters arrived before the sun was up. They kept coming through the morning, from north and south and east and west, in cars and dust-covered trucks, with notebooks and microphones and cameras. There were people from television, people from radio, people from newspapers as far away as Boston. There was even a fellow from *Life* magazine.

The sheriff was happy at first. He polished his star and posed with one foot on the front steps, his snakeskin boot all bright and shiny. But no one took his picture. They shouted, "Where's the boy? Where's the dog?"

Danny was in the jail cell, hearing all the clamor and commotion. He had Rocket at his side, the dog panting nervously. Danny heard the sheriff shouting back, "Just wait, okay? Just settle down, you hear?"

Every now and then the front door opened, and the

sounds from the street came in a louder burst and roar. In one of those bursts arrived the nice lady who'd brought him chicken the night before. Now she came with a breakfast of toast and scrambled eggs. She said hello to Rocket, then pushed the plate through the gap below the door.

"You're creating quite a ruckus, young man," she said. "There's someone out there from the *National Enquirer*? He's asking to see you. They're all asking to see you. They want to take your picture."

Rocket whined. Danny said, "They can't do that. They can't take our picture."

"Now, don't I just know that?" she said. "You sleeping here in the same clothes you've been wearing for days? You look a fright, but don't you worry, now. That's why the sheriff's waiting. Till I get you all cleaned up for your pictures."

"That's not what I mean," said Danny. If they took his picture, his parents might see it. But the lady was already gone. There was another burst of shouting as she went out to the street.

Then Alice came to see him. She came skipping down the stairs with her canvas bag swinging from her shoulder, her hair flying back. "Hi," she said. "You know you're famous now?" From her bag she took a newspaper from New York City and held it up for Danny to see the headline: "Mystery Boy Says Dog's His Brother."

"Your story got sent out on the wire," she said. "They're reading about you all over the place. From Kalamazoo to Timbuktu."

From the bed, through the bars, he glared at her. "You lied to me," he said.

"No, I didn't," said Alice.

"You promised not to tell anybody."

"I promised not to tell the *sheriff*," she said. "That's all. I was very careful about that."

She didn't look so pretty anymore, not to Danny River. She was like a fairy-tale witch who had come to him in the guise of a beautiful lady, and now he was seeing what she was really like. "You're mean," he said.

"Don't say that. I was just trying to help," said Alice. "What's wrong with your dog?"

Rocket's teeth were showing. He was half talking and half growling at Alice.

"He doesn't like you. He knows you tricked me," said Danny.

"Oh!" she said through the bars. "I was trying to save him, Danny. People won't let him be taken away from you now."

"You didn't even think about that, 'cause they can't stop it," said Danny. "It's only Creepy Colvig who matters, and now he's going to know where I am, and he's going to get Rocket. The police can't stop him; nobody can, except for Gus Grissom, but I won't ever get to the Cape thanks to you."

"Well, I'm sorry," she said, though she didn't *look* sorry, or *sound* sorry, with her words coming out like a snake's. "If they take him, I'll get you another dog, okay?"

Danny couldn't believe she would say such a thing, not after hearing his whole story. She hadn't believed a word of it; he could see that now. She had listened and nodded and pretended to believe him. He didn't know what "the wire" was, but he imagined his story riding the telephone wires, racing from pole to pole, from city to city.

"Did you get paid for the story?" he asked.

She was getting less pretty every minute. "Don't think I did it for money," she said. "I thought you'd be happy. I did it for you."

"Well, *thanks*," said Danny River. "Thanks a lot," he said, and turned away, his face toward the wall.

He didn't answer when she said goodbye. She said goodbye to Rocket, too, but the dog didn't move.

"So long, Rocket," she said again.

"Forget it," said Danny. "Dogs never say goodbye. They love to say hello, but they never say goodbye."

He heard her go up the stairs. A bell rang three times, and the teletype machine began to clatter and bang. It typed away, shaking the table, rattling like a machine gun. The bell rang again, and the machine whirred to a stop.

As though the teletype was a sort of mechanical rooster, it seemed to wake the office and the whole town with its bell. Telephones started ringing. Cars blew their horns. The reporters shouted more loudly, "Where's the boy? We want to see the dog."

Down to the cells came the nice lady and the sheriff together. The sheriff opened the bars and they came in. The lady gave Danny clean clothes—pants and socks, and a shirt in a cellophane packet. The sheriff was holding a torn piece of paper.

"Here's something interesting," he said. "A runaway from up north. Name of Danny River. Boy of nine years old, blond hair, in the company of a black-and-white dog. That sound familiar to you, *Beau?*"

"I never told you my name was Beau," said Danny River.

"Get dressed. You're going home," said the sheriff.

fifty-one

The phones were still ringing when Danny went up in his clean new clothes. The lady was talking on one, and the sheriff was on his radio, and the reporters were staring through the windows. A lady shouted, "There he is!" and cameras flashed, and lights brighter than headlamps glared in through the glass. Rocket stayed right at Danny's side.

The sheriff turned off his radio. He put a hand on Danny's shoulder and led him from the office as though they were father and son. On the little porch outside the door they stood above the crowd of reporters, and Danny saw that the street was choked with cars and trucks.

The reporters all yelled at once, all different things. Some of them cried, "Here! Look over here!" and others whistled so that Rocket would lift his head for a picture.

"Settle down!" shouted the sheriff. He held up both his

hands in a V above his head and turned slowly across the crowd.

There were stone lions crouching on platforms beside him. He lifted Danny and seated him on one of the lions' backs. The flashbulbs popped all over.

"This here's Danny River," he said. "And this here's his dog. And I'm Sheriff Eugene Brown."

"Are you going home, Danny?" shouted a reporter.

"Did you talk to Gus Grissom?" said another. "Did he call you?"

"Did your parents call?" said a lady.

"Now, we've had calls from all over," said the sheriff, his white eyebrows moving. "We've had calls from as far as California. From Canada. But the boy's tired, and he just wants to go home. You can say this in your newspapers and on your televisions: you can say the boy was put up for the night by Sheriff Eugene Brown, and now we're going to get him on his way."

They shouted back with more questions: Was he going to Cape Canaveral? What about Gus Grissom? Danny tried to answer, but the sheriff kept yelling, "No comment. No comment." One hand on Danny's shoulder, the other parting the crowd, Sheriff Eugene Brown took Danny to the police car. He put the boy and the dog into the backseat, then waved once more and drove away.

He started the siren. It whooped and whined as they passed through the town, toward the morning sun.

It was a very small town; in minutes they were out in the country, zooming down a gravel road in a cloud of gray. The sheriff kept the siren wailing, though the only thing they passed was a tractor. Danny saw the driver look down, startled, as the car went screaming past him.

Danny tapped the sheriff's shoulder. "Where are we going?" he asked. He saw the sheriff's lips moving but couldn't hear most of the words. *The city; your daddy; the Greyhound;* that was all he understood.

Rocket lay with his paws covering his ears. Danny put his hand on the dog's chest and felt him trembling. He imagined he was whining, but couldn't hear *that*, either. There was only the siren piercing through the car.

It seemed the sheriff was used to the sound. He still spoke on the radio, and must have heard when the radio spoke to him. Miles and miles from the town, he suddenly picked up the microphone, and his lips moved for a while. Then he looked back at Danny and spoke again.

"Pardon?" said Danny.

The sheriff flipped a switch that stopped the siren. "Change of plans!" he shouted, as though the thing was still blaring. "Brace yourself, boy."

There were no handles on his door. Danny barely had time to put a hand on the seat before the sheriff slammed the brakes and spun the wheel, sending the car skidding sideways down the road. In a crunch of gravel, it slid through half a circle. Then it straightened out, and the sheriff drove back through his cloud of dust. He turned on the siren again.

They swung left at a crossroads and went tearing north, enveloped by the dust. The car slid round the bends, and stones popped and crackled against the chassis. Danny had no idea now where he was going. For all he knew, the sheriff was taking him all the way home in that horrible howl of the siren.

Rocket's ears started twitching as they passed a herd of grazing cows. He jumped up to Danny's window, and a moment later, right beside them, appeared a yellow airplane, like a crop duster. It made Danny think of Steve Britain's little Skyraider going round and round Camp Wigwam. For an instant they seemed to be flying together, the car and the airplane, until the crop duster passed them. The sunlight flashed on its wings as it banked in a turn and settled to the ground.

It took the sheriff twenty minutes to reach the same place, an airport that seemed to sit in the middle of nowhere. He drove right onto the runway, then along its painted yellow lines, toward a block of buildings and a control tower that looked like a toy or a model. Along the sides of the runway, parked on the grass, were half a dozen private planes. Danny could see that one was a jet, with the name of an oil company painted on its tail, and he wished that Beau was there to see it. Then he laughed at himself, because Rocket was gazing at the airplanes, and in the black pools of his eyes Danny could see Beau staring out.

At last the sheriff turned off the siren. He parked the car and turned around in his seat. "I have to ask you something," he said. "This story you're telling, do you believe it?"

"Yes," said Danny.

"It's not just a tale to make yourself look important?"

Danny shook his head.

"Then why doesn't the dog do something?" The sheriff was looking at Rocket. "If he's what you say he is, and he's so darned smart, why doesn't he do something to save himself?"

Danny hadn't thought of that. He told the sheriff, "If you say his real name, he barks." But that didn't sound impressive even to Danny, and he blushed when the sheriff laughed.

"I'd think about that if I was you," said Sheriff Eugene Brown. He got out of the car and opened the door for Danny, and they all stood on the sun-heated runway. The yellow crop duster was being refueled in a halo of gas fumes.

"Why did you bring me here?" asked Danny.

"There's someone flying in to meet you, boy."

"In that?" asked Danny, looking at the yellow plane.

"No. In that." The sheriff pointed at the sky.

Danny looked up. There was a pinpoint of light moving above the fields, like a shooting star crossing the whole, huge sky. Rocket went crazy, spinning around in tight circles, barking and talking.

The light seemed to stop as it turned toward them. Suddenly it was hurtling right above them in a tremendous flash, in the wonderful roar of a jet engine. It changed in an instant from a speck of light to a white-painted fighter, then in an instant back again. It climbed straight up through the sky, winking like silver and diamonds, then fell and hurtled back. Again it passed above them, and on across the fields. It traveled in a moment as far as Danny could see, and the air was full of its fabulous, powerful sound.

People came out from the tower, out from the planes,

out from nowhere, it seemed. They stood in a group, all star-ing at the sky with their hands at their foreheads.

The fighter appeared in the distance, its three wheels hanging down, and it seemed to float above the field like a bird or a kite. It touched the runway and rumbled toward them, shimmering with the heat and the whirls of thin smoke from the jet. It stopped not a hundred feet away. The engine slowed to a whine, and then to a stop.

Rocket barked. He dashed toward it.

The plane was long and narrow, with a pointed nose and a tail like the fin of a shark. The wings were short, as narrow as knife blades, and half the plane stuck out in front of them. It looked to Danny like a big dart, and he knew right away—from Beau's models—that it was a T-38. Not entirely white after all, it had a blue stripe down its length, and a symbol like an atom painted on its tail. A long canopy bulged at the top, while the engines were nestled very close to the body.

Danny had never really marveled at airplanes, but this one looked beautiful even to him. It was like a strange bird that stood on three spindly legs, and it seemed as though it could hardly wait to lift those little legs and take to the sky again.

There were two cockpits, but only one flier. Danny could see him in the front seat, a man in a red helmet, his face covered with a mask. Rocket was right under the plane now, not tall enough to touch it even standing on his hind legs.

The canopy hinged open in two sections, each lifting up

and backward like the hood on Mrs. River's Pontiac. Seeing the glass and metal moving like that made Danny think of the plane as less like a bird and more like an incredible machine that must have come down through space from the distant stars.

The pilot lifted himself in his seat. He unfastened his mask and it swung free from one side, showing a face that was round and happy. He hoisted himself over the side of the cockpit and slid to the ground.

He was wearing a blue flight suit and a black parachute harness that jangled with its buckles. As Rocket leapt around him, he bent down to pat the dog's head. Then he walked toward Danny and the sheriff. Though he wasn't a big man, he looked enormously heroic to Danny.

He took off the red helmet, and his hair was black and short. He took off one of his thick gloves and held out his hand, grinning all the time with the friendliest smile that Danny could imagine. "I'm Virgil Grissom," he said. "They call me Gus."

Danny, of course, knew who he was. Who else could have come flying in to see him in this sparkling white machine? But he couldn't answer; he couldn't speak. Danny put his own hand into the hand of the astronaut, and he touched this man who had gone flying around the whole Earth in little more than an hour, again and again, who had seen the sun come up and the sun go down three times in a day, the only man in all the world who had been twice into space.

"You must be Danny River," this man said now,

squeezing Danny's hand. "It's a real pleasure to meet you, Danny. You're famous, you know."

Danny blushed. He giggled. Gus Grissom was among what Beau had called "the seven great men," and here he was telling Danny that *he* was famous?

"Holy man," said Danny. "Holy man, this is great, Mr. Grissom."

The astronaut laughed. "Gus," he said. "Okay?"

Then Danny remembered himself why he was there and what was important. He said, "This is Rocket."

"I figured it was," said Gus. "I read about him in the paper this morning. I've been hearing about him nonstop on the radio. But nobody said he's such a friendly little pooch."

"He isn't so friendly to everyone," said Danny. "It's just he knows who you are."

The grin never left Gus Grissom's face. It only grew wider. "He looks like my old Blackie."

Gus shook hands with the sheriff, then took Danny aside, to sit with Rocket in the shade of the airplane's wing. Rocket stayed right beside Gus, and Danny didn't mind at all.

"Soon as I saw the paper this morning, and your story right there on the front page, I said I had to meet that boy," said Gus. "I jumped straight into the T-38."

"Thank you for coming," said Danny. "Do you think you can save Rocket?"

That great, happy grin at last changed to something else. Gus looked at Danny and slowly shook his head.

"But you believe me, don't you?" said Danny. "That's

why you came, isn't it, Mr. Grissom?" He couldn't bring himself to say Gus.

Gus Grissom looked out at the runway and the fields. He squinted, as though the sun was shining straight in his eyes. "I won't lie to you, son," he said. "It was you I came to see, not the dog. I don't see there's much I can do there."

"You promised Beau you'd help," said Danny.

"That's your brother?"

"Yes. He wrote to you and you wrote back and said you'd help him if ever you could. You said if he came to the Cape you'd help him."

Gus was still squinting. He looked worried now, even ashamed.

"You remember that, don't you?" said Danny.

"No." Gus shook his head. He was holding his red helmet, turning it in his hands. "I don't live at the Cape, Danny. My home's in Houston."

"But the letter . . ."

"I never see those letters," said Gus. "There's some gals in an office take care of that. They send the same answer to everyone, son."

"You signed it."

"They have rubber stamps."

Danny blinked. He felt that hole in his stomach, and it was bigger and deeper than ever. It seemed almost funny that he'd gone so far and tried so hard just because a lady in an office had put a rubber stamp on a piece of paper. But it really wasn't funny at all.

Gus told him the same thing that Alice had said. He

told him that no one would take the dog away now. But he didn't know Creepy Colvig any more than Alice did. Poor Rocket understood it all; Danny could see that. Why, the dog was nearly crying, its eyes as wet as Danny's.

"What was it you hoped I would do?" said Gus.

"I don't even know," said Danny.

As they sat quietly below the wing, the sheriff came up to the plane. All the people who'd come from the tower were starting to gather round it, and he couldn't keep them back anymore. He walked right up to the T-38 with his snakeskin boots tapping on the runway. Then he bent down and looked underneath, and said, "I have to get going pretty soon."

"Can't I wait a little bit more?" said Danny.

"Got nothing to do with me," said the sheriff.

"But—"

"It's okay, Danny," said Gus Grissom. "I'm going to fly you home. You and your dog."

"Wow!" shouted Danny. "No kidding."

"Honest Injun."

"Holy smoke! Holy crow!" cried Danny. "You hear that, Rocket?"

The dog was leaping about, doing those quick twirls that nearly bent him double, talking a mile a minute. Gus Grissom watched him, and laughed. "Well, that's the darnedest thing," he said.

"Beau was always crazy about flying," said Danny. "He said there were only two things he wanted to do, and one was to fly in a jet."

"What was the other?" asked Gus.

"To float through space," said Danny.

"Well, we can't go quite that high," said Gus, with a chuckle. "But we'll go just as high as we can."

"Thanks," said Danny. "Thanks a million. I know you don't believe me, but—"

"No, I can't say that I do, son." Gus Grissom was grinning again. "But if *you* believe it, then I'm not going to argue. You knew your brother, and you know the dog, and it would sure be a swell old world if you were right."

"I am," said Danny.

"Let's get you suited up, son."

fifty-two

The T-38 sat high and level on its wheels. The nose was at the height of Gus Grissom's shoulder, well above Danny's head. He didn't see how he and Rocket could possibly climb into the cockpit.

But Gus brought out a thing like a handle, and when he fitted it into the side of the plane it hung down to make a step. A little higher, a second step hinged out from the fuselage.

Gus climbed up, and from the cockpit he brought down a flight suit like his own, and a helmet that matched his, and a parachute with its harness. He helped Danny into the blue coveralls. "That's John Glenn's old suit," he said. "He's not real huge, so it might fit you." He hung the parachute on Danny's shoulders, then squashed the helmet on his head.

Danny stood there with the sleeves of the suit rolled up

to his elbows, its legs in huge bundles at his ankles, his helmet flopping on his head. He imagined he looked like a real astronaut, like one of the seven great men. Then Gus said, "You look like one of the seven dwarfs," and that punctured him a bit. But Gus smiled with such friendliness that Danny laughed with him.

Gus boosted him to the first step, and Danny managed from there, though he nearly tangled himself in the parachute. He clambered into a seat that was gray and hard, with only a small blue cushion. His feet straddled the control stick, and all around were gauges and dials and switches. He had thought once that his father's septic truck was the neatest thing in the world. Then he'd seen Cody's truck and thought it was so much better. But this made even Cody's big rig look like one of the silly plastic cars on a kiddies' merry-go-round.

Gus stood on the step and, leaning under the canopy, settled Danny into the seat. He fastened belts around his waist and shoulders, then raised the whole thing as high as it would go, hoisting him up with the whirr of an electric motor.

Next he got down and fetched Rocket. He slipped the dog right into Danny's flight suit, then drew up the zipper so that the boy and his dog were bundled together.

"Now, I got Gordo to rig this up, him and Deke Slayton," said Gus, as though they were just two ordinary guys and not half god, half man. "They did the best they could with a few minutes' notice." He fished out, from the side of the seat, an oxygen mask for Danny. Spliced into its hose was another hose, joined in a big knot of duct tape that was silvery gray. It made a V of hoses, with two masks—one for Danny, and a smaller one for Rocket. Gus plugged it into a fitting, attaching hoses and cables. "Your pooch won't need it most of the time; we'll stay low," he said. "But when I tell you to, you'll have to put this over his nose, you understand?"

"Yes," said Danny.

"Now, he won't want to wear it, I guarantee that. He'll do any old thing to shake it off," said Gus. "But without it he can't breathe up there. And he has to breathe, Danny. Like you or me."

"It's okay. He understands," said Danny. "He won't mind wearing it."

Gus laughed. "Try it out."

There was a thin strap on the mask. It was far too big for the head of a little dog, so Gus tied a big knot that made it shorter by half. He gave the mask to Danny, and Rocket lowered his head, as though waiting for it to be slipped over him. He didn't whine and he didn't growl; he just sat bundled in Danny's suit and let the mask be put on his nose.

"Now, that beats all," said Gus.

Danny adjusted the rubber so that nothing covered Rocket's eyes. Gus showed him how to start the oxygen, and Rocket breathed his normal breaths.

"Well, that's some dog, I have to say." Gus patted Rocket's head, then explained to Danny some of the controls and gauges. "It's all identical to what's up front," he said. "Between your legs, right in your way there, that's the stick. You'll see it moving when I move mine. Push it left, we bank left. Push it forward, the nose goes down. Try to keep your hands off it, Danny. If you need something to hold on to, grab that handle there."

He pointed to the gauges right in front of Danny. "The artificial horizon," he explained, tapping the biggest dial, right in the middle. "It shows if we're banking or climbing or what." On its left was the altimeter. "That tells our height," said Gus. "Now, this one gives the speed in knots, and that one there's just a fancy clock." His hand was moving quickly now, and wherever he pointed, Rocket was looking. "The rest of these you don't have to worry about. Now, there's just one thing I'll get you to do, Danny. You'll have to pull out the pin in the ejector before we taxi. That's right here." He leaned across Danny and made sure the boy put his hand in the right place. "You see? It slides out real easy."

From the buildings around the control tower, a man drove out in a truck with a great big box on its back. He parked right in front of the T-38 and pulled out a long, thick hose that was just like the one on Old Man River's septic truck.

"Is he pumping us out?" asked Danny.

Gus gave him a funny look. "That's the starter truck, Danny. It's going to blow air through the engines to get them turning." He ruffled Rocket's hair and tapped his knuckles on Danny's helmet. "Happy flying," he said, and closed the canopy.

Gus Grissom got into the front seat. He put on his

helmet and mask. He talked to Danny through the intercom. "Okay?"

"Okay!" said Danny.

The man from the truck vanished under the T-38 with the long hose. The big box on the truck was an air compressor, and it made a terrible din and a rattle. Then Danny heard the jet engines turning. They whined and hummed, then started.

The man came out, dragging the hose. He stood beside the wings as Gus tested the controls. Danny watched the control stick waggle back and forth. He saw the rudder pedals moving beyond his feet. His legs weren't long enough to reach them.

The man stuffed the air hose beside the compressor and drove away in the truck. Through the intercom, Gus said, "Danny, pull out your pin now. Hold it up so I can see." Then he taxied the T-38 toward the tower and turned it around.

The back of Gus Grissom's red helmet and the instrument panel blocked Danny's view. He had to tip sideways to see much of anything out of the front, and Rocket was doing that now. But Danny could look out the sides, and with the wings behind him he could see nearly straight down at the ground.

The engines turned more quickly, more loudly.

"Hang on, Danny," said Gus in the intercom. "You'll feel a bit of a push."

A bit of a push! It was like his father leaping from a

stoplight in the Pontiac, but it went on and on without stopping. It pushed Danny back in his seat, and pushed Rocket against his chest, and the runway sped by, and the little airplanes and the hangars, and the people who'd come to watch. In only a moment Danny traveled faster than he'd ever gone in his life. Then the control stick moved backward, and the T-38 lifted into the air with a pull at his stomach. It tipped its nose high and went blasting up above the fields with the engines making a deep and pleasant whoosh that beat steadily all around him. He saw houses shrink to specks, and whole fields to little patches. Next the control stick moved sideways, and the jet leaned over, and it pushed him down in the seat as it swung around to the north.

"How you doing?" asked Gus.

"It's great," said Danny into his mask.

"And Rocket?"

"Man, he's loving it."

Yes, Rocket was loving it. His eyes were sparkling with that look of pure joy, his mouth open and grinning. He looked out through the canopy, and down at the controls, and up at Danny and licked his face.

"You want to go higher?" asked Gus.

"You bet."

They climbed nearly straight up. Danny watched the altimeter as they passed ten thousand feet. Twelve thousand feet. Now all the little patches of fields looked as small as the houses had looked. Still they went up, straight up to a blue sky. Fifteen thousand feet. Twenty thousand. Twenty-five thousand feet.

"Better give the dog some air," said Gus, and Danny put the mask on Rocket's nose. "Tell me when it's on."

"It's on," said Danny.

Gus chuckled. "Afterburners, Danny. Another push."

Into the steady sound of the jets came an extra little swoosh. Again Danny felt the seat shove at his back. He saw the airspeed indicator nudging up to five hundred knots. The altimeter moved steadily. Thirty thousand feet. Thirty-five thousand feet.

The air was changing color, growing darker. At forty-five thousand feet, Danny was looking up at a black sky. He could see the moon and the stars in the daytime, the bright band of the Milky Way right above him, and still they were climbing. To either side and below him, the world stretched to huge horizons.

At fifty-three thousand feet, Gus said, "We're ten miles up."

Danny could see Rocket's eyes staring above the edge of the oxygen mask. They were bright as stars themselves, with a funny glow in this strange light at the edge of space. He whispered into his own mask, "You're doing it, Beau. You're getting what you always wanted."

Then the T-38 leveled off, and the engines slowed. Now it really felt to Danny that he was floating in space. If he didn't look down, there was no earth. It was only dark blue sky beside him, stars and the moon above.

"That's Saturn high on the left. Mars on the right," said Gus in a quiet voice. "It's really something, isn't it, Danny."

Danny nodded. He didn't have words to say what it was like.

"I'd live up here if I could," said Gus. "Who needs the world, eh, Danny? Who needs all the troubles on the ground?"

They flew for long minutes up there, hurtling over cities and counties. Danny was shocked when he looked at the airspeed dial and saw that they were blasting through the sky at six hundred miles an hour. It felt as though they were standing still. He hugged his dog so tightly that he nearly squeezed the mask from Rocket's nose. He could feel now that Rocket was happy, and that whatever happened next, when they returned to the troubles on the ground, the dog wouldn't mind. Beau had gone floating through space.

Gus rolled the airplane on its back. The big dome of the canopy filled with nothing but the blue and green of Earth. He rolled it right around and upside down again, the world becoming space, becoming world again. They started down.

"Watch your altimeter there," said Gus.

Danny stared at the dial. He saw the meter quiver and swing.

"We've busted through the sound barrier," said Gus. "We're going faster now than the speed of sound."

They kept dropping, plunging toward the ground until they were again at ten thousand feet. Then Danny took off Rocket's mask, and the dog licked his cheek.

"Do you want to fly her, Danny?" asked Gus.

"Can I?"

"You bet."

Danny put his hands on the control stick. He could feel a heaviness in it, and knew that Gus was still holding it, that he wasn't really flying the jet himself. Gus told him to pull it back. "Gently," he said.

Danny pulled. The nose shot up, and the T-38 leapt a thousand feet. He pushed the stick instead, and the nose went down. He banked to the left; he banked to the right. Then he flew straight and level above green forests and a river. He saw Gus Grissom lift his arms and press both his palms to the glass of the canopy, and Danny's heart did a turn as he realized he was actually flying. When Gus took the controls again, they did a loop and a roll, and they went tearing off to the west because Gus saw a thunderhead there.

So they shredded through the clouds at a speed faster than sound, and tore out through their tops, and dashed along canyons and mountains of clouds.

Before Danny really knew they were heading there, he was home. Gus brought the plane to a beautiful landing at the airport not five miles from Hog's Hollow. It touched its wheels on the ground; then the nose lifted up, and the drag of the air slowed it down.

They taxied to a stop. Danny looked out through the canopy at his mother and Old Man River.

fifty-three

Mrs. River ran to the jet in her long dress and flat shoes. She was there when Danny came out—down a real ladder that a man in a jumpsuit clipped into place. She laughed at the sight of Rocket poking his head from the flight suit. Then Rocket jumped free and welcomed her with barks and bounces. Mrs. River hugged Danny as tightly as he had hugged Rocket.

"Oh, Danny," she said.

The Old Man came more slowly, his keys jingling. Rocket met him ten yards from the airplane and leapt circles around him all the way back. Then Old Man River tugged his cap and smiled at Gus, and swept Danny right off the ground in his arms.

Danny was still in his helmet and flight suit. The blue arms and blue legs came free from their bundling, and they flapped around Danny as the Old Man swished him back and forth.

"We went into space," said Danny. "Right to the edge of space."

"Well, don't you ever dare do it again," said Mrs. River. "Don't leave us, Danny."

"It's been terribly lonely without you," said the Old Man.

"We did a loop! We did rolls!" cried Danny. "We went up ten miles, and I flew it myself. I flew the plane, Dad."

"That's great," said his father.

Gus Grissom was standing beside the T-38, holding his red helmet with his gloves pushed inside it. He looked shy, just a happy, shy little man. He was much smaller than Old Man River but seemed pleased that he fairly towered over Flo.

"This is Gus," said Danny.

Both his parents shook Gus Grissom's hand. Mrs. River even hugged him, and that made the astronaut's ears turn red. "It's an honor," said Old Man River. "I can't thank you enough."

"My pleasure. Really," said Gus. "That's a fine boy you have there."

"I know," said the Old Man. "I've been blessed with wonderful sons." He pulled his cap and added, "The older one had an accident. You probably know all about it."

Gus mumbled that he did.

"You were his hero, Mr. Grissom."

"Oh, not really. Not me," said Gus. "It's just the man in the spacesuit that kids come to admire. Heck, there wouldn't even have to be a man inside it. It's just the suit and the helmet. It's the job."

"No, it was more than that."

The two men looked so uncomfortable that Danny cringed to see it. The Old Man looked away and said, "Beau worshipped you."

Then Gus looked the other way and said, "Yes, I know. He told me."

Danny's heart did a somersault. He thought Gus had come to believe the whole story and now would convince the Old Man, who was already frowning at Gus. Then the astronaut laughed again and said, "I mean it was Danny who told me. The dog didn't say a word."

The Old Man chuckled. "Oh," he said. "I thought he had you believing it. Such a crazy thing."

"Not really," said Gus with a little shrug. "It's maybe not so crazy." He helped Danny take off the parachute. "You wouldn't believe the sort of ideas I've had up in space. From a hundred miles up, this world's like a big blue marble. You look down on it, and you start thinking how amazing and incredible it all is, and . . . I don't know." He set the parachute in a heap. "Up there, you believe in things you wouldn't believe on the ground, Mr. River."

They both looked at Rocket, who was sitting now— pleased and proud—in the shade of the T-38. His tongue hanging out, his tail wagging, he looked like any dog.

Gus pulled the helmet from Danny's head. "You see the whole world as a miracle. That's what I'm saying. You see there's more to it all than any one person can ever understand."

fifty-four

The Rivers and Rocket stayed on the runway until Gus flew away. They watched the T-38 lift into the air, and saw it turn and come back. It passed low above them, dipping its wings, and Danny saw the red helmet of Gus Grissom behind the canopy glass.

They all waved—or all except for Rocket, who was wagging his tail furiously—and they were still waving and wagging when the airplane was a speck climbing into the sky. Then they walked together to the Pontiac and started off for home.

Danny kept listening and watching for hints of what would happen next. But his parents sat silently, in that way that made time feel like glue. So he talked about Rocket.

He told them how Rocket had kept quiet in the transport truck, how he'd acted with the sheriff and Alice and all the reporters, how he'd bounced around Gus Grissom, and how he'd sat so patiently with the oxygen mask. It sounded to Danny as though his words were falling into a hole. He could feel that his parents didn't want to hear it but didn't want to stop him.

They drove into Hog's Hollow, down the winding road. They didn't have to cross the big bridge, not coming from the airport. They followed the twisting road, and Mrs. Elliot was looking out her window.

The Old Man waited until the very last bend, until he was turning the wheel. Then he said, "You can't keep him, Danny."

The road straightened. There was a police car parked outside the old gray house. There was a policeman leaning against the door.

It was the same short policeman from before, but now he was alone. He was waiting by the road when Old Man River parked the Pontiac.

"No!" cried Danny. "Go away!" But the policeman only moved nearer to the car, until he stood so close to the window that Danny could see no higher than his fourth button.

"Dad!" shouted Danny. "Mom!" No one answered. "Oh, Rocket." He grabbed his dog and held him.

Old Man River gripped the steering wheel as though the car was still moving. "Danny, give him the dog," he said.

"No!" shouted Danny.

His mother turned around. She'd been crying—maybe all the way home; Danny didn't know. She said, "If you don't give him the dog, he'll arrest your father. He's got no choice."

The only one to say sorry was the policeman. He spoke with his head hidden by the roof. "Danny, I'm sorry. I really am," he said. "I read your story in the paper this morning. If it was up to me, I'd let you keep the dog."

That made the Old Man furious. He shoved his door open. He leapt out. "And if it was up to *me*, what do you think *I* would do? Do you think I'd break my son's heart, you piece of—"

"No, sir, of course not," said the policeman. "I'm only doing my job, sir."

"Then *do it*," snarled Old Man River in the most terrible voice that Danny had ever heard. "Do it and be damned!"

"Charlie!" cried Mrs. River. "Oh, great balls of fire, this is horrible. Danny, please. Please just get this over with."

"I can't. I can't," said Danny, weeping.

The Old Man pulled the back door open. He came halfway through it, his head and shoulders, and Danny slid away across the seat, pulling Rocket with him.

"Listen, son," said Charlie River. "If there was a single thing I could do, I'd do it. I swear to God, Danny."

"Call him by his name," said Danny. "Look in his eyes and call him Beau."

"Oh, Danny, *please*."

"You'll see," said Danny. His throat felt fiery. His lips tasted tears. "Call him Beau and you'll see."

The Old Man reached out his hands to take the dog.

Danny held him back, but Rocket squirmed away. Rocket left Danny for the Old Man's arms.

Charlie River lifted the dog from the car. He held it up and looked in its eyes but didn't say a word. Rocket was whining very quietly. Then the Old Man turned and handed the dog to the policeman. Rocket struggled a bit, but not very much. His whines become more of a wailing, and his round eyes gazed at Old Man River.

Danny struggled from the car. "Let me hold him," he said. "At least let me say goodbye."

The policeman hesitated. But he looked wretched—they all looked absolutely wretched. He held out his arms and let Danny take Rocket. "A minute," he said. "Only a minute."

"Leave me alone with him," said Danny.

"I can't do that," said the policeman.

Danny sat on the ground; he slumped to the earth. He let Rocket stand up beside him, and the dog seemed to be hugging him. He could see the feet and the legs of the people waiting around him—the policeman's and his father's, and his mother's, too, as she came from the car.

Danny whispered into Rocket's ear. "Run away," he said. "Run far away, and don't come back."

He turned the dog around and shoved its hips. "Run!" he shouted.

"Don't do that!" said the policeman.

"Go!" shouted Danny.

Rocket ran, but only twenty feet. He turned and wagged his tail. The policeman stepped toward him, and when he was very close—only then—Rocket turned and ran again. He went another twenty feet, and there he waited a second time, his tail swishing slowly, like the plastic cat's on the kitchen wall.

Danny remembered that Rocket had done this before. Now, with the same dashes and darts, the dog led the policeman, Danny, Charlie, and Flo up through Hog's Hollow. The words of Sheriff Eugene Brown came into Danny's mind: *If he's what you say he is, and he's so darned smart, why doesn't he do something to save himself?*

Rocket led them up the winding road nearly to its end. He led them to the house of Creepy Colvig.

fifty-five

When Rocket reached the Colvigs' lawn he made one more dash—down the side of the house and round its back.

The policeman and the Rivers went in a tight little group and found him there. He was digging in the grass. He was flinging dirt and grass in a spray of brown and green. He turned and dug again in the same place, and his claws began to scrape on something hard.

Creepy Colvig came out of the house in his undershirt, down the steps, yelling at them all. Danny could hear Dopey inside, calling in his howls and grunts.

"What are you doing?" said Creepy, barreling over the grass. "Why is that damned dog still here?"

Rocket bared the top of Creepy Colvig's septic tank. He scraped with his claws at the ragged edge of the concrete lid.

"He wants to open it up," said Danny. He hurried to help, but Creepy Colvig pushed him aside.

"Keep your hands off my son!" shouted Old Man River.

"Then get him out of my goddamned garden," said Creepy. "All of you get out."

The policeman held up his hands. "Just calm down. Everyone calm down."

"Look in the tank," said Danny. "He's trying to show us something."

Old Man River found a shovel leaning against the house. It was the same shovel that Creepy had given to Danny so long ago, to scrape broken glass from the street. The Old Man spat on his hands and pried with that shovel to lift the lid of the septic tank. The block of cement fell back, and he dropped the shovel and peered inside. He put his hands on his thighs and bent forward.

"This is nuts. This is goddamned nuts!" shouted Creepy Colvig. He yelled at the policeman. "Why are you letting this happen?"

"Be quiet!" said the policeman.

Charlie River was trying to divine something from the contents of the septic tank. He tilted his head to the left, then to the right. Rocket barked beside him.

Old Man River picked up the shovel again. He worked the blade through the hole, then swished it round in the tank. He stopped and looked again. He swished once more and raised his head.

"Danny, I'm sorry," he said. "I'm so sorry, son."

"Charlie, what are you talking about?" said Mrs. River.

Nobody knew what the Old Man meant, or why he was suddenly apologizing. They watched as he twisted the shovel. Then, carefully and slowly, he drew it out through the hole. Sitting on the metal blade, balanced at the very edge, was a little plastic missile.

"That was Beau's!" cried Danny. "It's from the Rocket Base."

The Old Man nodded. "Now, how did it get there? That's the question." He tipped the shovel, and the missile fell off onto the grass.

Danny told again how Beau had been killed. He remembered running over the mountains of dirt, chasing the missiles from Beau's favorite toy, the Rocket Base USA. "We were playing a game. Just playing," he said. "Then Dopey came and—"

But the proof was there on the grass. The missile was lying there, and Rocket was sitting beside it, mewling in his talking voice.

Old Man River, who had never believed Danny's story, now saw that he'd been wrong. The policeman understood, and even Creepy couldn't deny it. "He said he wasn't there. He swore he wasn't there," he said, looking around from person to person. "When I seen him with that thing, I didn't know what the hell it was. I thought he'd found it somewhere; that was all. I never let him keep them things. I flush them away; I flush them all away."

Old Man River was fishing again with the shovel. He

plunged it through the sludge and scraped the blade on the bottom, down the side of the tank, into the corner. When he raised it again there was a twisted bit of chrome on the blade, and half of a pair of little scissors rusted through at the hinge.

"He likes shiny things," said Creepy Colvig. "He sees something, he takes it. But he's harmless, really. He's harmless."

Danny felt sorry for the man. He didn't want to, but couldn't help it. Creepy was pulling at his shaggy hair, standing there with his potbelly swaying. "He didn't mean nothing that day. He wouldn't have known what he was doing," said Creepy, turning from the Old Man to the policeman to little Flo in her long dress. "Look, I'll forget about the dog, okay? You keep the dog. Just don't take my boy away. He's all I got. He doesn't know what he's doing."

Danny went over to Rocket. He reached down and petted his dog. The day of Beau's accident came into his mind as clear as a movie. He saw Dopey appear at the edge of the pit, and all that happened afterward. "It was an accident," he said. "Dopey came and stole the missile, and we were teasing him with it, like monkey in the middle. Then Dopey rushed at Beau, and . . . What happened, it was just an accident."

Creepy stood alone in his filthy undershirt in the middle of the garden. "I didn't know he was there," he said. "I swear I didn't know."

Old Man River came and got Danny and Rocket. He led

them toward the street, guiding Danny with a hand on the boy's shoulder. He said, "Let's go home."

"What about Rocket?" said Danny.

"That's over now," said Old Man River. "Don't worry, Danny. It's *all* over now."

fifty-six

For the rest of that summer, and the summers that followed, it was again a happy family that lived in the old gray house in Hog's Hollow. It was a family of four to Danny, but to everyone else it was a family of three and a dog. He once caught the Old Man staring into Rocket's eyes, just staring down into those big brown eyes as he held the dog's head in his hands. But Danny never saw that again.

The Colvigs moved away, as they'd moved so many times before. Once again, Danny could wander wherever he wanted, up and down the trails, over the little bridge, always with Rocket behind him.

Not two years later—in January of 1967—he came home from school to find his mother in tears. "Oh, Danny," she said, as she hugged him. "I just heard on the news; Gus Grissom, he's . . . ." She sniffed and started again. "There was a fire on the launchpad, Danny. Gus; he . . . he burned to death." Rocket had come bounding in with Danny, wagging and leaping, his eyes full of sparkles. But now his tail drooped, and with a whimper he settled to the floor. Mrs. River looked at the dog, and then at her son, and it was a moment that Danny would remember forever. She believed in him then; he could see that she did. If only for that one instant, she believed that Beau was back. And in that speck of time, in the saddest hour of a sad day, Danny had never been happier.

But the years passed. As Danny River grew older, as he watched Rocket grow older, he began to wonder about the things that had happened during that Gemini summer. He began to wonder if what he had come to believe was really true.

There were times when he thought Rocket was only a dog, and no more than a dog, and those times came more and more often as the summers went by. He thought once in a while that maybe Beau had left again, that he'd come back only for those few magical months. But at other times, even when Rocket was getting rather old, Danny could still look into the eyes of the dog and see his brother behind them. And at those times he remembered looking up from the edge of space, and the dog's black eyes were like the endless darkness he'd seen from the very top of the world's blue sky.

He came to believe that maybe there were things in the world that only children could understand, and that as long as he thought that a boy could die and live again as a dog, it would be a swell old world after all.

Acknowledgments

As a child in Toronto I often rode a bus through Hog's Hollow, where the main street of the city dipped through a big valley. To the west, the land rose and dipped again, into another valley "one holler over," as my friend from the Ozarks would say. This second hollow didn't have a name. We called it the ravine. There was a road that curved down from the busy street, under a bridge, and into the valley. At one end lay the golf course and the toboggan run of Killer Hill. At the other end was a tangle of trails, leading up to a summer camp where boys played at being Indians.

This is where Danny lives, in a neighborhood pieced together from places and people I used to know, including a man like Creepy, who made me crawl around on the street to pick up the bits of a broken bottle, and a kid like Dopey, who attacked me with a realtor's sign. So the small details of Danny's life are true, but all the rest is made up.

For that huge part of the story I would like to thank those who helped with the research and writing:

Kathleen Larkin of the Prince Rupert Library answered questions about the Mercury and Gemini space programs and put me in touch with various experts. Her sister Patricia Larkin-Lieffers located film footage of the space flights, while her niece Caroline Liefers watched hours of video and recommended the best of the NASA clips.

Margaret Persinger, of public affairs/multimedia at the Kennedy Space Center in Florida, provided videotapes of NASA films. Kandy Warren, contact center manager at Kennedy Space Center, sent videos and set up interviews.

Roger Zweig, a test pilot for NASA, described wonderfully and patiently what it's like to fly in a T-38. He and Larry Glenn, a NASA flight engineer, took photographs that let me put little Danny right into the cockpit of one of the jets.

Charles Early and Sarah Endres of the Goddard Space Flight Center Library helped with research into television coverage.

Randall Brooks, curator of the physical sciences and space at the Canada Science and Technology Museum in Ottawa, shared his recollections of watching the early space flights in junior high school.

Smith Wells, a truck driver and my brother-in-law, explained the workings of transport trucks, then corrected my many mistakes about air horns and air brakes and Jake brakes.

Deputy Kroger of the San Bernardino County Coroner's Office explained the procedure for the investigation of accidental deaths.

David Dodge, astronomer at the H. R. MacMillan Space Centre in Vancouver, BC, and NBC reporter Jay Barbery pointed out errors in my accounts of the Mercury and Gemini space missions.

Veterinarians Thomas Uhlig and Patricia Leather of Gabriola Island explained the treatment and care of runaway dogs, and the problems of puppies at high altitude.

Scott Grissom talked to me briefly about his father, Gus Grissom. I hope he's pleased with the story.

David Froom of Island Septic Services of Gabriola Island explained the job of a septic-pumping man, and made it sound so exotic that it changed this story.

Finally, I'd like to thank those who read the manuscript along its way and made it so much better: Bruce Wishart, Kristin Miller, Raymond Lawrence, and especially Françoise Bui, and all the others at Random House.

About the Author

Iain Lawrence grew up in the Canadian cities of Toronto and Calgary. There was often a dog in his family, very often a cat, and for a while a monkey. He lives on the Gulf Islands of the West Coast and has sailed many times up and down the Inside Passage, always with a dog as part of the crew. This book is dedicated to one of those dogs—the Skipper—who made the trip fifteen times.

Iain Lawrence's previous novels for younger readers include the High Seas Trilogy: *The Wreckers, The Smugglers,* and *The Buccaneers*; and *Lord of the Nutcracker Men*. His novels for young adults include *B for Buster, The Lightkeeper's Daughter,* and *Ghost Boy,* as well as the companion books *The Convicts* and *The Cannibals.*

You can find out more about Iain Lawrence at www.iainlawrence.com.